THE WESTPORT WILD ONES

Trace had always heard that Westport, Connecticut, was the home of the super-straight-arrow citizens of America's eastern gold coast.

Then he got there.

First he ran into the guardian of a sweet little old lady—a fellow who looked like a gorilla but didn't act quite as civilized as one.

Next he had an encounter of the closest kind with a beautiful lady next door who was in fevered competition to outscore her husband in the infidelity game.

After that he visited a doctor whose favorite means of relaxation was sitting naked in a hot tub with a glass of ice-cold champagne in his hand and an overheated blonde nurse by his side.

By this time Trace figured that no one in this terrific little town could surprise him—until a killer did. . . .

TRACE
ONCE A MUTT

SIGNET Mysteries You'll Enjoy

TRACE
ONCE A MUTT

WARREN MURPHY

A SIGNET BOOK

NEW AMERICAN LIBRARY

For
Nevins, our friend in Densa

PUBLISHER'S NOTE

This novel is a work of fiction. Names, characters, places, and incidents either are the product of the author's imagination or are used fictitiously, and any resemblance to actual persons, living or dead, events, or locales is entirely coincidental.

NAL BOOKS ARE AVAILABLE AT QUANTITY DISCOUNTS WHEN USED TO PROMOTE PRODUCTS OR SERVICES. FOR INFORMATION PLEASE WRITE TO PREMIUM MARKETING DIVISION, NEW AMERICAN LIBRARY, 1633 BROADWAY, NEW YORK, NEW YORK 10019.

SIGNET TRADEMARK REG. U.S. PAT. OFF. AND FOREIGN COUNTRIES
REGISTERED TRADEMARK—MARCA REGISTRADA
HECHO EN CHICAGO, U.S.A.

SIGNET, SIGNET CLASSIC, MENTOR, PLUME, MERIDIAN AND NAL BOOKS are published by New American Library,
1633 Broadway, New York, New York 10019

First Printing, April, 1985

1 2 3 4 5 6 7 8 9

PRINTED IN THE UNITED STATES OF AMERICA

Westport, Connecticut—The death of Helmsley Paddington, inventor of a string of pet products, was revealed today in papers filed in Superior Court here.

According to the brief filed by attorneys for Mrs. Nadine Paddington, the widow, Paddington, who was then 37, died seven years ago when his private plane crashed somewhere between New Hampshire and Newfoundland.

Paddington, a licensed private pilot, was on his way to Newfoundland to join in a protest against the killing of baby harp seals for their fur. At the time of his death, the couple were living in West Hampstead, New Hampshire.

Mrs. Paddington, now a resident of Westport, Connecticut, asked the court to officially declare her husband dead, even though his body has never been found.

1

Devlin Tracy said, "Well, well, so Helmsley Paddington died. What a shame."

Tracy was a big, blond rumpled man who held a large brandy snifter of rosé between both hands. He was talking to Walter Marks, vice-president for claims of the Garrison Fidelity Insurance Company. Marks was barely five feet tall and he wore pin-stripe suits and elevator shoes in an unsuccessfully desperate effort to look taller. He had small hands and manicured fingers and he had that slightly distracted air of the chronically finicky, as if he were always looking around for something to dust.

It was obvious from the way his thin lips curled that he did not like Devlin Tracy.

"You know about Helmsley Paddington?" Marks said.

"Never heard of him," Devlin Tracy said. "But I remember seven years ago, I woke up one night and all I could hear was dogs howling. It was like they were howling all over the world. At first I thought it was a werewolf UFO, but it wasn't because nobody came to rip my throat out. Just dogs howling. I finally went back to sleep, and when I woke up in the morning, they had all stopped. That must have been the time Paddington's plane crashed. Dogs know things like that. Earthquakes too." He waved to the waiter for another drink.

"Maybe you were just drunk, Trace," said Walter Marks.

"That's a possibility. I was drunk a lot then, as I remember," Trace said.

"You're drunk a lot now," Marks said. He looked as if he were smelling something bad.

"No, no, that's totally different," Trace said. "Back then, I drank hard stuff, vodka, and I drank it all the time. I was committing suicide. I'm surprised you never tried to stop me. One would almost think you wanted me dead."

"And how is that different from now?" Walter Marks asked.

"Now I drink only wine," Trace said. "This is very good for your body because it prevents waxy buildup in your arteries. I may live forever."

"God, what a prospect," Marks said.

"I don't know. I look forward to immortality with glee," Trace said.

"Well, you still drink too much. I don't care if it's wine or vodka or bird's-nest soup. You still always look like you have a buzz on."

"There are reasons for that," Trace said. "It's not like it's something I want to do."

"How's that?"

"I read this story about how high alcohol levels in the blood protect you against nuclear radiation. Those of us who believe in mankind have a responsibility to preserve the race. Do you know how awful I feel when I see all these people walking around, unprotected? It's shameful. Don't people care that they might be the last person left in the world and the whole future of the race depends on them? Drink, Groucho. Mankind is counting on you."

"As long as noboy's counting on you," Marks said stiffly. "Let's get down to business."

"I'm all ears."

"I want you to look into this Paddington case."

"Why?" Trace asked.

"Because he was insured by Garrison Fidelity for a million dollars. With an accidental death, this Mrs. Paddington gets two million."

"Accidents happen," Trace said with a shrug. "Pay up." He surrendered his empty glass to the waiter and started drinking from the full one. Marks waited until the waiter left before he spoke again.

"Not accidents like this," Marks said. "Not like he dies and she doesn't say anything for

9

seven years. I had one of the researchers check the indexes. Not a word in the paper for seven years about these people. Not a word."

"Dead men don't talk," Trace said. "That might explain it."

"I don't believe it," Marks said. "You think there would have been a rumor, a buzz from somebody, a question. 'What happened to Mr. and Mrs. Poop?' That kind of thing. Why have they left the public eye?"

"Paddington, not Poop," Trace said.

"No. They called them Mr. and Mrs. Poop. That was like a joke because he kept inventing these things to pick up dog crap or something. Christ, he makes a zillion dollars out of dog turds. What kind of a world is this?"

"Look at the bright side," Trace said. "If he didn't, the world would have been knee-deep in dog droppings. You'd be neck-deep."

"Please save your short jokes for somebody else," Marks snapped. "So, anyway, there hasn't been a mention of these people for seven years and now all of a sudden she's got a lawyer and she wants us to give her two million dollars."

"Ah, why not?" Trace said. "Make her day. Send her the money."

"Because I don't believe in any of these missing-at-sea things and seven years later, whoops, he's dead, pay up."

"What do *you* think happened?" Trace said.

"I think this is a scam," Marks said. "Just like they always are. I think this Paddington guy is living in an abandoned mine shaft someplace and every weekend he comes up and stays in a motel twenty miles outside town and porks his wife and they're having a big laugh at our expense. That's the way it always is."

"You seem to have your mind made up already," Trace said. "Why bother me with it?" He turned away from Marks and asked the bartender for a cup of Sanka.

The bartender looked at Marks quizzically, but the insurance-company official shook his head no, sourly, as if annoyed at being disturbed.

They were the only two customers sitting at the long bar. It was chillingly cool, but through the front window, the men could see the summer heat shimmering up from the pavement of the Las Vegas Strip.

"This whole thing will be in court in a couple of weeks," Marks said. "We want to be ready before then, and know how this Mrs. Paddington's trying to cheat us. It's right up your alley. An easy one for you."

Something in the tone of his voice made Trace suspicious. He thought silently for a while, then said, "You've had somebody else working on this, haven't you?"

Marks looked up with an expression of hurt astonishment. Trace just glared at him, and finally Marks said casually, "Well, we had somebody else take a quick pass at the case. Just a light sweep, if you will."

"And?"

"And . . . Well, he didn't find out anything," Marks said.

"I don't believe you, Groucho," said Trace.

"What don't you believe?"

"I know you. You don't hire anybody to take a quick pass at anything worth two million dollars. You had teams of damned investigators digging into this thing for—what's the date on the clipping?—right, for two months and they've come up with zilch and now you want to give me this dead end with a couple of weeks left so that if I can't find anything either, you can blame it on me and tell the world how incompetent I am."

"You really astonish me, Trace," Marks said. "I'm giving you a job. That's all. A job. Why do you always try to make it a matter of personal animosity between us?"

"Because it is. Because you hate the fact that Bob Swenson is my friend, so you can't fire me because the president of the company likes me. So you keep giving me these rotten jobs and trying to make me fall on my face. It's what you always do."

"I'm hurt. I came to give you this job because I thought you could use the money. You usually can."

"Not anymore. I'm on my way to being independently wealthy," Trace said. "Did you notice? I'm drinking Gallo wine now. I'm moving right up. No more wine in cardboard barrels. It's all first class from here on in."

"Rich relative die?" Marks asked.

"Nothing that good," Trace said.

"You haven't gone and actually put money into one of your lunatic business schemes, have you?" Marks asked. He shook his head. "Not that CB bible of the air? Or those backward signs for the fronts of cars? Or making Oklahoma into a parking lot?"

"Tulsa, not Oklahoma," Trace said. "And you'll rue the day you declined to invest in them. But, no, to answer your question, this is something totally different."

"Such as?"

"I've invested in a bar and restaurant," Trace said.

Marks laughed aloud. "You'll drink up all the profits, if there are any."

"This restaurant's three thousand miles away. Oceanbright in New Jersey. You know it?"

"Shore town?" Marks asked.

"Right. Right on the ocean, and so's the restaurant. A friend of mine is going to run it and I own a piece."

"What kind of return are you getting?" Marks asked.

"The money's going to start rolling in any

day now," Trace said. "You know how traffic is every Friday night getting out of New York?"

"Yeah?"

"Well, all those people are going to the Jersey shore. To Oceanbright. To my restaurant. Every one of them. I'll tell you, I'm going to be swimming in wealth."

"Did you know that the highest failure rate for new ventures is in the restaurant business?" Marks said. "Seventy-five percent of all new restaurants fail."

"You just made that up," Trace said. "You're trying to ruin my day and make me work for you."

"No, it's a true statistic. My lawyer told me. Somebody tried to get me to invest in a restaurant and he checked it out for me."

"Who'd want you in a restaurant?" Trace said. "You'd scare all the customers away."

"They wanted my money, not my charm."

"I hate you, Walter Marks," Trace said. "You have a knack for making everything banal and dirty."

"I'm just trying to be helpful," Marks said. "Try to get your money back before it's too late."

"This restaurant is going to be one of the ones that succeeds. It can't miss, I tell you."

"Well, I wish you luck. Honestly, I wish you luck."

"I'll make believe that you mean it," Trace said. "So you understand why I can't take this job for you."

"I really don't. Even if your restaurant pays off, which I doubt, you'll still have to have some money coming in."

"I'll get by. The restaurant's opening real soon and I expect a big check from them any day. And in the meantime, I've still got my retainer from you people."

"You're turning me down, then?" Marks said.

"Absolutely."

"I don't know how we can justify continuing to keep you on retainer when you won't provide any services," Marks said.

"What do you mean by that?" Trace asked.

"You're an accountant, you should understand."

"I used to was an accountant. Now I are an entrepreneur," Trace said.

"You can still understand. We pay you a retainer so that you're available when we need you. If you're not going to be available anymore, then we can't justify paying you a retainer, can we?"

"This is my life you're messing around with," Trace said.

"I, for one, hope you get wealthy and famous in the restaurant business," Marks said.

"If you come into my restaurant, I'll give you

the appetizer free. But not the shrimp cocktail. That's fifty cents extra."

"Okay. Let's leave it at that, then," Marks said.

"You're very gleeful about this, Groucho," said Trace.

"Trace, let's be honest about this. You don't like me and you don't like working for me."

"I wouldn't say that."

"What would you say?" asked Marks.

"I'd say I hate you and I hate working for you."

"Okay," Marks said. "I'll go along with that. And you are not exactly one of my favorite people either. So I think it's not such a bad idea that we come, like this, to an amicable parting of the ways, so to speak."

"You're happy to be rid of me, aren't you?" Trace said suspiciously.

"Yes. I would say that."

"Well, I'm not quitting yet."

"You don't have to quit. You just have to decline to work. That's what you're doing."

"Do you want to get rid of me two million dollars' worth?" Trace asked.

"Two million? Oh, that's if you could find any fraud or anything wrong with this Paddington case. Detectives, real detectives haven't been able to find anything wrong."

"If there is something wrong, I could find it," Trace said stubbornly.

"We'll never know that, will we?" Marks said. "Now that you're a restaurant tycoon."

He left a few minutes later, smiling uncharacteristically. Trace stayed behind at the bar.

2

When Trace got back to his condominium apartment on the Las Vegas Strip, he noticed the number seventeen in the little window on his telephone-answering machine.

Either a lot of people had called him today or else he hadn't looked at the machine for a long time. He poured a glass of wine from a jug in the refrigerator and sat down to ponder which was the more likely event.

Seventeen messages? All in one day? It seemed highly unlikely because he didn't know seventeen people. He finished the wine and poured another glass. He looked at the sunset behind the hills in the distance. It would have been beautiful if he hadn't realized that behind those hills, California lurked.

Seventeen people? Let's see. There was his

mother and his father, but his father didn't call and his mother only called at hours when Trace would normally be in bed so she would be sure to reach him and be sure to disturb his sleep. Jaws, his ex-wife, never called, and their two kids, What's-his-name and the girl, never called either, which was exactly as he wanted it. Bob Swenson, the president of Garrison Fidelity Insurance Company, might call, but usually only if he was in a jam. That was about it.

Chico, Trace's roommate, might call, but it wasn't likely because she knew that Trace was untrustworthy and was rarely in the apartment.

Therefore, Q.E.D. The seventeen calls must have come over a period of time. Days, weeks, maybe even months. He didn't remember when was the last time he looked at the machine. He didn't even know what his telephone tape message sounded like.

Maybe he had tried to reach himself? Would he call seventeen times, thinking he could find himself in? Not even if he were really drunk would he do that. And since he had cut down on his drinking, he rarely got really drunk anymore. He just kept enough of a buzz on to protect himself against nuclear radiation. He had convinced himself that this was very important, living in Las Vegas, where the sun shone all the time and the air was very thin.

He wondered what his message sounded like. He reached over to the tape machine and pressed some of the unfamiliar buttons and heard tape whirring and clicks and he didn't know what any of it meant. Then he pressed another button and was rewarded by the sound of his own voice reciting his recorded message.

"The number you have reached is not in service. Please do not call again. Thank you for your consideration."

He pressed another button that he thought would rewind the message so the machine was ready to operate again. It wouldn't do for the telephone to ring and for him to have to answer it while he was busy drinking wine. He hated to be disturbed when doing something important. When the restaurant started to pay off, he would probably take the phone out, he thought. Anybody who wanted to reach him would have to show up on his doorstep like a supplicant and he would leave orders for the concierge downstairs to throw everybody out. Refuse admittance to anyone who didn't have an appointment. And he would make no appointments before their time.

He was holding down the button that he thought would rewind the tape, but it didn't work. He released the button and heard another voice on the machine.

"Trace. This is Eddie. I've got to talk to you about the restaurant."

Eddie. Eddie was his main partner in the restaurant at the New Jersey shore. Maybe he had some money already for Trace. That would teach Walter Marks. If Trace were rich before Marks even left Las Vegas, that would show him, with his spread-gloom attitude.

Trace fumbled around in the little drawer of the telephone table looking for a cocktail napkin with Eddie's phone number on it. When he found it, he called the number in New Jersey.

"This is Trace."

"I'm glad you called back," Eddie said. "Did you hear what happened?"

"No. Where's my share of the profits?" Trace said.

"We're not even open yet. What profits?"

"Then there's nothing good that's going to come of this phone call, is there?" Trace said.

"Afraid not. You didn't hear what happened?"

"No."

"Last night we had a storm."

"We didn't," Trace said. "It was nice here. Sunny all day, evening temperature in the high sixties. It was beautiful."

"I wish it was that way here. We had a storm like you never saw."

"Why are you giving me a weather report?"

"It's important."

Trace knew something was wrong because he was starting to feel sober. "Go ahead," he said. "What happened?"

"The goddamn ocean came up and overflowed the place. We've got a lot of storm damage."

"Spread newspapers. Blot it up," Trace suggested.

"Can't do that. We've got real damage. I had a contractor in today to look at it."

"How much?"

"It looks like it's going to cost fifty, sixty thousand dollars to fix."

"You're not asking me for money, are you?" Trace said.

"Of course I am. All the partners have to kick in some money. That's the only way we can fix this place up and open up on time."

"How much?"

"You're a twenty-percent partner. I need ten, twelve thousand dollars from you."

"I don't have it," Trace said.

"Get it. We need it to do the repairs."

"What do you think, I'm made of money?"

"So we've got to pinch a little. We all do. When we get this restaurant rolling, the money's going to come pouring in."

"The only thing pouring in right now is the freaking ocean," Trace said.

"Well, that's the way it goes."

"When do you get the insurance money?" Trace asked.

"What insurance money?"

"For the damages."

"No insurance. It's an act of God."

"Bullshit," Trace said. "It's an act of water."

"The insurance company won't pay. They don't do that down here."

"I hate insurance companies," Trace said.

"*You* work for one, not me. Why do you do that anyway?"

"Because I've been trying to change them from within," Trace said. "It just hasn't worked yet."

"If it had, we wouldn't have to put up this extra dough," Eddie said. "When do I get your check?"

"A check I can send you right away. Ten thousand dollars I don't have."

"I want a good check," the other man said.

"I hate you," Trace said. "When the hell is this restaurant going to open?"

"We've been delayed a little bit by the storm damage."

"How little's a little bit?"

"A month or so."

"Are we going to miss the summer season down there?" Trace demanded.

"Not if you send me the twelve thousand," Eddie said.

"Ten thousand," Trace said.

"With room to grow. Send it right away," the other man said, and hung up before Trace could say anything more.

In order, Trace hung up the telephone, removed the modular plug from the answering machine, threw the machine in the kitchen garbage can, refilled his glass with wine, and sat down to try to figure out where to get ten thousand dollars with room to grow.

When Michiko Mangini unlocked the door to the apartment and entered, two unaccustomed sounds assailed her ears.

Trace was singing and something was sizzling in the kitchen.

She looked down the length of the long living room toward the small kitchen at the rear of the apartment. Trace stood with his back to her, at the stove, singing an operatic aria at the top of his voice. As usual, he remembered only one line of the aria, so he sounded like a stuck record as he sang it over and over again.

"*Di quella pira. Di quella pira. Di quella pira. Di quella pira. Di quella pi-i-i-ra. Di quella pira. Di quella pira.*"

"Is that fire for dinner? What are you doing?" the young woman asked. She was twenty-six years old, small and shapely, with blue-black hair and soft dark Oriental eyes that looked bottomless in the shiny taupe of her healthy young face.

"*Di quella pira. Di quella pira. Di quella pira. Di quella pira.*"

She shouted. "What are you doing?"

Trace turned with a big smile. He put down a pot he was holding.

"Hello, Chico. What I am doing is cooking

dinner for my honey. Did I ever tell you I love you?"

"I'm not lending you any money," Chico said and went into the bedroom to change.

Later, as they sat at the small kitchen table and drank coffee, Trace explained, "It's not like I'm trying to borrow money from you."

Chico had thrown out Trace's halting attempt at dinner, something he called a sardine souf-flé, and had instead cooked them steaks and asparagus and green salad. Trace had little appetite and only picked at his food, but Chico didn't mind because she ate both his and hers.

"It's not like I'm trying to borrow money from you," he said again. "Dammit, *respondez-moi*."

"Oh? Then, what is it?" she asked sweetly. She took a piece of cake from a small plate in front of Trace and bit off a large wedge.

"I hate the way you eat," he said. "What is it is that I'm giving you an opportunity to get in on the ground floor . . ."

"Along with the ocean," Chico said.

"Will you listen? Levity is not called for here," Trace said. "This is a big financial deal we're talking about. I'm going to make you rich."

"Hah," she said. Crumbs sprayed from her mouth. She picked them up from the table and ate them.

"Moving right along," he said. "I'm allowing

you to buy into a New Jersey restaurant. One of the hottest places on the shore."

"It's not even open yet. How the hell hot is that?" she asked.

"It will be. And for fifteen thousand dollars, a mere fifteen thousand dollars, you can have half my share."

"For which you paid forty thousand dollars," she said.

"That's right. Every cent I had in the world. I paid forty thou and now I'm willing to give you half for just fifteen thou. This is a real good deal. This restaurant's going to make a fortune."

"If it's such a sure shot, why are you selling it off in pieces?" she asked.

"Because this is a way for you to get financial security, for all your days. And it's only going to cost you fifteen thousand."

Chico shook her head, caught a dislodged crumb in midair, and nibbled it from her fingers.

"No," she said finally. "I don't trust the restaurant business. Did you know that seventy-five percent of all new restaurants go foldo?"

"Yes, I knew that. That's why I investigated this one so thoroughly before I invested in it."

"Investigate? Thoroughly? That lunatic friend of yours called, and before you were off the phone you were sending him all your life savings. You've never even seen the place."

"I know the town. Oceanbright is beautiful. The restaurant can't miss."

"It'll miss, Trace. You're in on it, it'll miss."

"Come on. Half my share for only fifteen K. You could sell it on the open market for more than that."

"You think so?"

"I know so," Trace said.

"Then, why don't you just take your half-share and sell it on the open market? You can do better than the fifteen you want from me."

"Because I want to do something for you. Because you are the light of my life and I can't bear the thought of you working while I live a life of leisure. Don't you see, I'm doing it for you?"

"You want to do something for me, take the garbage out to the incinerator. Your wine jugs make it too heavy for me to lift."

"Let me be sure I understand this," Trace said. "You're going to pass up this opportunity?"

"You understand it very well," Chico said. "I pass."

"How about lending me some money, then?"

"No."

"Why not?"

"You're not good for it," she said.

"I'm going to have to raise your rent here," Trace said. "I never thought it would come to this."

"What's my new rent going to be?"

"Fifteen thousand dollars a month," Trace said. "Payable one month in advance."

"I'll move. Then, where will you be?"

"The whole world's against me," Trace said.

Chico retrieved the telephone-answering machine from the garbage can, plugged it back in, and rewound it to zero. All the other messages had been for her.

She dressed in a russet cocktail dress and told Trace she had some business, which meant she was doing a favor for the casino and "entertaining" some out-of-town high roller. As she left, he pointedly said nothing, but merely turned up the volume on the stereo.

After a couple of drinks, he called Robert Swenson, the president of Garrison Fidelity Insurance Company. It sounded as if Swenson was having a party because there was a lot of screaming and shouting in the background, almost enough to drown out Swenson's big avuncular voice.

"Hello, Trace. How's Chico?"

"Mean, avaricious, and deceitful, as usual. Why don't you ask how I am?"

"Because you're fine. You're always fine," Swenson said.

"What the hell is all that racket?"

"Let me close the door. Okay, what's on your mind?" Swenson said.

"Did you talk to Walter Marks today?" Trace asked.

"Yes. He told me you were quitting."

"I never said that," Trace said. "What'd you say?"

"I said good riddance to bad rubbish," Swenson said.

"Thanks a lot, pal," Trace said.

"You don't want to quit?"

"I never said I was going to quit. I was just turning down one assignment and Groucho made it into a big deal, like he was taking me off retainer and didn't need me anymore and like that. Do you think I'd quit and leave you?" Trace asked.

"Yes," Swenson said. "As soon as you got two nickels to rub together."

"Well, it's not like that at all," Trace said. "I'll tell you this. I want to do that job in Westport."

"What's their names? Paddington? The guy who died in the plane crash?"

"That's right. I want to do that job. For you, Bob. And for the company."

"That's the worst bullshit I ever heard in my life," Swenson said. "What's the matter? Broke again?"

"That's not important. I just want to do that job for you," Trace said.

"If that's the way you want it."

"But I can't call Groucho and tell him I changed my mind," Trace said.

"Why not?"

"I couldn't bear the humiliation of it all," Trace said.

"So you want me to call him and tell him to order you to take that job?" Swenson said.

"Something like that. But you could tell him to ask me nicely. He could plead a little bit."

"Trace, he needs a little stroking now and then too. Let him order you. It's good for his undersized ego."

"All right. As a favor to you, he can order me."

"Anything else?" Swenson asked.

"No, that was it," Trace asked. "You never told me what that racket was."

"Oh," Swenson said. "I've got a few friends over. The wife's out of town."

"Swell," Trace said sarcastically. "I'm going through a crisis and you're giving parties."

"Crises come and go," Swenson said. "But parties are forever."

It was almost daylight when Chico returned and walked quietly into the bedroom.

Trace didn't ask her where she had been or what she had been doing. He knew and didn't care to think about it. She spent a long time in the bathroom, then slid into the bed alongside him.

Without rolling over, he grumbled, "If you'd invest your money wisely in a New Jersey restaurant, you wouldn't have to supplement your income this way."

"Get off it," she growled.

"Don't come begging to me later," he said, "because I'm withdrawing the offer."

"Good. I'd hate for it to always be between us."

"I'm going east tomorrow," Trace said.

"Why?"

"I've got a job for the company."

"I thought you turned it down," she said.

"I changed my mind."

When Walter Marks called in the morning to order him to take the Paddington case, Trace was already packed.

He said, "Okay, Walter. I'll do it for you. As a favor."

"Just do it," Marks said sourly.

When Trace went downstairs to get a cab to the airport, Chico was still sleeping.

He left a note on the kitchen table. It read, "I hope you know what I'm going through, trying to make our old age secure."

3

When Trace arrived at Kennedy Airport in New York, a man was waiting outside the gate, holding a hand-painted sign over his head with the name "Devlin Tracy" hand-lettered on it.

Trace ran up to him and snatched the sign away, crumpled it, and dropped it to the ground.

"Hey, what you doing?"

"My ex-wife. She's got spies everywhere," Trace said. "If she knows I'm in the East, I'm as good as dead."

"You Tracy?"

"That's right."

"Here." The man pushed forward a manila envelope. "They told me at the insurance company to deliver this to you."

"No chance it's filled with money, is there?" asked Trace.

"No. It's reports or something."

"Well, thanks, I guess," Trace said.

As he waited for his bag, he looked around occasionally to make sure his ex-wife wasn't lying in wait for him. It wasn't that he owed her money; his alimony and child support were always paid precisely on time. It was because every time he ran into her, she wanted to talk.

"Look," he had said once. "If I wanted to talk to you, I would have stayed married to you."

"This concerns the children."

"They're no concern of mine," Trace said. "You spawned them, you take care of them."

"They need a father," Cora had shouted.

"Well, rent one, for Christ's sakes. Just leave me out of it."

And that had ended the conversation. He had found it very satisfying because she had gone a full six months before trying to contact him again. But you could never be too sure, so he checked the people waiting around the baggage area.

From time to time, he glanced into the manila envelope the messenger had brought him. It seemed to contain a thick file on Helmsley and Nadine Paddington. He folded it and stuck it into his back trouser pocket.

After retrieving his bag, Trace walked over to the car-rental office, where he had to take a number and stand in line, as if he were in a bakery on Sunday morning.

He hated car-rental companies. They were always advertising things like "One week, $119, no charge for mileage," but after you got through with everything, the car cost you $98 a day and had a soft right rear tire. As close as he could figure out, the special $119 weekly rate was only for visiting diplomats who booked six months in advance.

When he got to the head of the line, the car-rental clerk asked him, "What kind of car would you like?"

"A blue one," Trace said.

"I don't mean that. I mean compact, intermediate, or full size."

"You got a Stutz Bearcat?"

"Very funny," the clerk said.

"Well, if you don't have that," Trace said. "I'll take anything. As long as it's blue. And none of that crappy sky-blue either. I mean a real dark blue."

Fifteen minutes of paperwork later, as he surrendered the keys, the clerk said, "Would you mind telling me why you have to have a blue car?"

Trace said, "Because blue cars never get stopped by the cops. You watch from now on. You'll never see a dark-blue car pulled over at the side of the road."

This, to Trace, was absolutely, indisputably true. That the rental clerk shook his head in disbelief didn't change the facts; it just meant that the clerk was a fool. And who but a fool would work for a car-rental company? Of course, it took a bigger fool to work for an insurance company, he reminded himself sourly.

Westport, Connecticut, a hundred minutes away, didn't have a hotel, not a real one with many floors and elevators and candlelight dining on the top floor, so Trace had called to reserve a room in the Ye Olde English Motel.

He hated motels. He was forty years old and many years had passed since motels had been fun, since they had represented a warm bed, a warm body, and a warm farewell. And usually, a quick head-down walk through the parking lot so no one would see the woman's face.

Now he was more interested in room service, and motels never had any. He was interested in talkative bellhops, and motels didn't hire bellhops. He was interested in finding his room waiting for him, but motels always told you that the room wasn't ready yet and if you would just wait four hours in the lobby, they would have it done right away.

And now motels had computers. Trace was convinced that computers were the biggest time-waster that the hotel industry had ever been inflicted with. It used to be that when he reserved a room, he just had to show up, sign the registry, and let them take a print of his credit card. Now, a clerk took his name, then spent endless minutes having the computer search for vacancies in the motel's south wing, then north wing, then rooms with a view, and then finally announce that Mister Devlin Tracy had not made any reservation and there were only sixty-three rooms available but he couldn't have any of them. Computers might make some things work smoother but motels weren't among them.

Trace had had the good sense to stop at a liquor store on the Post Road for a bottle of Finlandia. It was evening and he had already chalked the day up as a total loss, so he took off his clothes and sat in the chair by the window looking out over the highway, and read the file that Walter Marks' office had compiled on Nadine and Helmsley Paddington.

Mrs. Paddington had been born Nadine Grand in Honolulu, the only child of a career naval officer and his wife. Her parents had died in an automobile accident while the family was living in Tampa, Florida, and Nadine was a senior in high school.

She had no other relatives and lived alone for the remainder of the school year. Then she sold the family home and used the proceeds, and the military insurance her father carried, to send herself to Great Britain to study at the Royal College of Veterinary Medicine.

There she met Helmsley Paddington. He was a native of Minneapolis and his parents too had died just a few years before. According to one of the Xeroxed news clippings enclosed, he was an Eagle Boy Scout but no great scholar. He spent his summer vacations from school working on a dairy farm and as a volunteer at the county's animal shelter. He wound up in Great Britain after having won a scholarship from the Minnesota 4-H Clubs for outstanding community service.

Neither graduated from veterinary college. Instead while they were both in their second year, they invented a device for turning dog droppings into compost, efficiently and without odor. The Doo-Right, the name they gave it, was a great success in a land of dog lovers and subsequently throughout the world. It led to a string of pet products marketed under the Paddington name.

The couple married and stayed in England for ten years, then moved to West Hampstead, New Hampshire, where they lived in a big estate on a lake. Their home was called Paddington's Com-Pound and was filled with dozens of dogs of every description.

When he first saw the thick pile of newspaper clippings, Trace thought that the Paddingtons were simply publicity hounds, but reading them changed his mind. It was true that the Paddingtons had vigorously courted publicity, but in each story about them, they managed to insert a strong endorsement for kindness to animals and a commercial for whatever cause they were promoting that day.

They loved animals, they said, pure and simple. They raised money to stop the slaughter of the harp seal. They gave money to save dolphins, to save seals, to stop research vivisection. They headed up an effort to stop the sending of live animals into space, calling it "cruel and unusual" punishment.

Trace shook his head and poured another drink. Apparently humans didn't count, he thought, because there was no effort on the Paddingtons' part to stop people from going into space.

After reading the clippings, Trace thought there must have been as many reporters as dogs at the Paddington Com-Pound most of the time. But if there had been any friction between the couple, none of the stories showed it. Invariably, the Paddingtons were described as inseparable, held together by love and their commonality of interests, and as much as Trace wanted to dislike them, because he thought that all zealots were nuts and these two obviously had won degrees in animal zealotry, the stories always showed an honest, sincere, and loving couple and he found himself liking them.

And then the stories had stopped. The last big interview was dated 1978 and the clippings after that, instead of being full-blown feature stories, were more often on the order of a single paragraph that said basically that the Paddingtons had become reclusive, or that the Paddingtons could not be reached for comment.

One of Walter Marks' legal beagles had done some research into the Paddingtons' wealth. When they left England, they had sold their interests in the Paddington Pet Line to a small conglomerate, Metrogeneral, Ltd., in return for shares of stock.

On paper, the stock deal had made them rich because their shares were worth on the open market approximately three million dollars and dividends alone amounted to more than two hundred thousand dollars a year.

But seven years earlier, just about the time of Paddington's disappearance, Metrogeneral stock had taken a beating. The price of its shares had dropped by 90 percent and it had stopped paying dividends.

The Paddingtons, the financial report said, still held their shares of Metrogeneral stock.

What it meant, the report said, was that the Paddingtons' three million dollars in shares had shrunk in value to about three hundred thousand dollars; and their regular dividend income of two hundred thousand dollars a year had been turned off when Metrogeneral cut out paying dividends.

Unless the Paddingtons had saved a lot of money, Trace thought, it meant that the couple might well have been facing a sharp financial pinch.

He thought about that for a while as he re-filled his vodka glass. He hated the plastic glasses he found in most motel bathrooms. And there were never ice cubes to be found. Still, warm vodka in a plastic glass was better than no vodka at all, and it tasted especially good after months of trying to make it on just wine.

The last item in the folder was a letter from Adam Shapp, an attorney, in Westport.

The letter read:

> Claim is hereby made for payment of policy number AF12425848 in the amount of two million dollars.
>
> On October 17, 1978, the insured, Mr. Helmsley Paddington, of West Hampstead, New Hampshire, disappeared while on a private flight from that town to Newfoundland. No word has been received from him and this office has petitioned the Superior Court of the State of Connecticut to officially declare Mr. Paddington dead of accidental causes.
>
> We call for payment of the policy on behalf of Mrs. Nadine Paddington, the widow, now resident in Westport, Connecticut, who is represented by our firm.

Trace leafed through the thick pile of papers again to see if he had missed anything, and found a sealed manila envelope.

Inside was a one-page report from C.S. Brunner Investigators, who had been hired by Garrison Fidelity to look into the Paddington story.

The report said that the plane did take off as reported from the lake in West Hampstead, New Hampshire, where the Paddingtons lived, neighbors having heard the motors revving up.

The Paddington plane was on its way to Newfoundland, a distance of slightly more than five hundred miles, where Paddington was planning to take part in a protest against the slaughter of the harp seal. The plane, a twin-engine Cessna seaplane, never landed, and no wreckage was ever spotted.

At the time of the flight, however, there was a heavy storm in the Atlantic and the normal path of the plane would have taken it right through that storm.

"There is no indication," the report said, "of there having been any trouble between Mr. and Mrs. Paddington, and it is the conclusion of this office that Mrs. Paddington's claim is valid."

That was the entire report, and Trace felt good thinking about Walter Marks spending good money for detectives who wound up telling him to pay up.

He celebrated by topping his glass with more warm vodka.

Idly, he looked through the clippings at the reproduced photos of the Paddingtons. Helmsley Paddington had been a tall, thin man who looked very tweedy in the photographs, even in those where he was wearing jeans and an old army shirt and wrestling with some of his dogs. He had an open, uncomplicated face with thinning mud-colored hair.

Nadine Paddington stood next to him in most of the photos, and it seemed to Trace as if she were trying consciously not to smile. She was a pleasant-looking, regular-featured woman with ashy blond hair, and wide-set intelligent eyes.

But why didn't she smile?

Another picture showed why. Mrs. Paddington had a mouthful of teeth that splayed out at a forty-five-degree angle from the vertical. With teeth like that, he wouldn't have smiled either.

He tossed all the newspaper clippings onto a pile with the other papers, then carried his glass to the bed and lay down to smoke. The ashtray was already filled and he mumbled to himself about motel ashtrays always being designed for nonsmokers or for people who smoked one cigarette every six days. He hated that.

Actually, he hated everything right at the moment, most of all being in Westport, having to look into the Paddington case when the guy was dead. All he was doing here was trying to figure out how to steal ten thousand dollars from Garrison Fidelity for a fee so he could pay for the restaurant's repairs.

It was all Chico's fault.

If she would have parted with some of her

ill-gotten gains, he wouldn't have had to do this. He could just have stayed in Las Vegas, waiting for the restaurant profits to come rolling in. His friend Eddie expected the restaurant and bar to gross three million dollars the first year, with a half-million of that as profit. That meant that Trace, as a 20-percent owner, would make a hundred thousand dollars as his share.

And against that, he'd be able to write off his taxes the depreciation of the building and the purchase of new equipment and a lot of other stuff, and why didn't Chico understand that he was on his way to Easy Street?

No, she was tight, so tight she squeaked. And she had no vision. That was what was wrong with Michiko Mangini. She had no vision, no way to see the big picture.

She lived in a world of petty mortals. She would never understand his dreams. She would never fly. She would always walk. Sometimes she might walk fast, but it would still be walking.

He thought he smelled something burning. He saw that the ashtray, filled with butts, was smoldering. He stubbed out the cigarette he was holding, then tried to use the butt to put out the other burning cigarettes. But they were slipperier than eels, and all he managed to do was push them out of the low-sided flat ashtray onto the bed. He burned his fingers trying to pick them up. Finally, he got them all together and took the ashtray inside the bathroom and flushed its contents down the toilet.

Then he took the plastic wastepaper basket from the bathroom and under the tub faucet ran an inch of water into the bottom. When he was satisfied it didn't leak, he brought it back and stood it on the floor next to his bed.

He looked at it and it made him more miserable than before. It was like being back in the army, sleeping in a barracks, with a butt can filled with wet sand hanging from a nail. A community ashtray.

He was forty years old and here he was, lying in a motel room, using a water-filled garbage can as an ashtray. Why not crystal? Waterford. Baccarat. It was all Chico's fault. She had reduced him to this by her parsimony.

He got up and in the Formica-topped desk in the corner of the room found a postcard that showed a picture of the motel in hideous Technicolor. The dogwood trees had been in bloom when the picture was taken and it looked bright and cheerful. Trace knew he had missed the dogwood season by three months. All he was going to have was July sweat and exhaust from trucks passing the motel on the Post Road.

He addressed the card to Chico and in the space for a message wrote: "Dear Chico. You will never soar. You will always only walk. Trace."

He looked at his message approvingly. Already he felt better. Striking back was always good for depression. If I'm not near the one I hate, I hate the one I'm near. Was that a song?

He read the message again, aloud this time. Its words seemed nasty and trivial to him.

Good, he thought. That's what he wanted to be, nasty and trivial.

Inside his wallet, he found a corroded old twenty-cent stamp that he had taken from a *Time* magazine renewal notice and put it on the postcard. Then he left his room to walk over to the motel's lobby to find a mailbox. He hoped the mailbox was inside the cocktail lounge.

He wanted a drink with ice.

4

A heavy iron gate closed with a chain and a padlock separated the Paddington home from the rest of the world. Trace thought it was probably to protect the world from the maniacal packs of curs that roamed the grounds day and night.

He parked his car alongside the high stone wall next to the gates, but heard no dogs barking, and when he looked through the gates, he saw no dogs anywhere in the sloping lawns that led up to the house.

He saw no people either, and he looked around for a bell or buzzer. Finally he found a button almost buried in the cement that anchored the gate into the stone walls. He pressed the button for a long time but could not hear it ringing anywhere and still saw no one at the house, which was set back fifty yards from the gate behind a roadway wide enough for two cars.

He kept pressing the button. Finally he stopped and shouted, "Hey. Is there anybody alive in there?"

There was still no answer, so he tried the button again and then shouted some more.

Maybe he could go over the wall. Sure. And Mrs. Paddington could pick just that moment to let her hundred starving Dobermans out for a walk. No, thank you. Maybe an air drop. Maybe he could get a helicopter to set him down on the Paddington roof.

He leaned on the button again and then shouted again. Maybe he should have telephoned first.

The garage was open and Trace saw two cars parked inside: one was gray; the other, a foreign station wagon, was red.

Then he saw a man coming out of the garage and walking slowly down the driveway. He was wearing a T-shirt and blue jeans and he was fastening his belt as he came toward the gate. Trace would never have called the expression on his face one of unalloyed joy. On the other hand, he might not have called the thing on the front of the man's head a face either. The skin was red and the jaw jutted forward. His brow sloped back into a hairline that had probably receded from embarrassment because his hair was black and knotty. While his face was sharp-featured, nothing seemed to go with anything else, and if people wound up looking like their pets, this man kept vultures. In a long-ago adolescence, he had probably suffered from acne—although, Trace thought, "suffered" was the wrong word. People suffered from acne when other people made fun of them. That had never happened with this person. Even when he was not around, kids would have said, "Yes, Gargantua, yes, he has real nice skin. And a sweet gentle disposition. Gargantua is the salt of the earth." He probably never even knew he had acne. Maybe he thought everyone else was wrong and who was to say nay?

The man was as big as Trace and he had the sloping shoulders and stringy arm muscles of the very strong, who don't have to lift weights to prove it.

Trace put his age at around forty but wasn't sure because he had very little experience with Cro-Magnon man.

He had a scowl on his face. Somehow it made him look more appealing than having blood dripping from his mouth, which Trace thought was the most likely alternative. His eyes, fixed on Trace like a marksman's sights, were beady.

Trace reached under his jacket and turned on the small portable tape recorder that he always carried, taped to his skin under his shirt.

He waited until the man was almost at the

gate and then reached over and hit the buzzer button one more time for good measure.

He smiled at the man, who did not smile back.

"That isn't funny," the man said. Even his voice was menacing, low-pitched, soft and hissing as if he spoke only on the inhale.

"Sorry," Trace said. "I was ringing the bell so long it just got to be a habit."

"People oughta watch their habits. Some of them aren't healthy."

"But some are very healthy," Trace said. "For instance, I'm in this habit of taking two hours of karate training every day. Now, that's what I call a good habit. You never know who you might meet."

"Never know," the man said, and sipped air. "I'm in the habit of carrying an ax handle myself, for just the same reason. What do you want?"

"That's neat," Trace said. "Hardly anybody in my crowd carries clubs anymore."

"What do you want?" the man said.

"I want to see Mrs. Paddington."

"You have an appointment?"

"Not exactly," Trace said.

"Then you can't exactly see her."

"Why not?"

"Because she doesn't see a lot of people," the man said.

"Maybe she'll make an exception in my case," Trace said.

"Why should she?"

"I'm from the insurance company. Something about two million dollars," Trace said.

The man paused. Trace promised to remember that for the future: mentioning a couple of million dollars had a way of catching people's attention and bringing civilization to the provinces.

"You wait here," the man ordered. "I'll see if she'll see you."

"I'll wait," Trace said. As the man walked away, Trace pressed the button again. Trace couldn't hear it, but obviously the man could because he wheeled around and glared at Trace.

"Sorry. Just fooling around," Trace said.

"You fool around too much."

"Well, paaaaardon me," Trace said.

While he waited for the man to return, he wondered how he was going to come up with ten thousand dollars. He had no illusions about earning anything except his expenses on this case and Chico seemed intransigent. He had no savings left and there wasn't much he could do to cut down on his life-style and make it less costly. He looked at the cigarette in his hand. Maybe he could switch to generic cigarettes, the kind they sold in supermarkets in those black-and-white packages that made them look like poor people's beans.

He discarded that idea right away. He had smoked a generic cigarette once. It was a moment he would never forget because it had answered a very large question. Trace had been thinking that there should be a way to recycle horse manure from racetracks. Supposedly it was good fertilizer, so why didn't every racetrack in America have a manure-processing plant built right next door to it? He had thought it was only shortsightedness, and then he had smoked the generic cigarette and it was suddenly obvious that there was no need for manure-processing plants because racetracks had found something else to do with horse manure. They sold it to companies to make generic cigarettes.

Another brilliant idea shot to hell. He looked at his cigarette and threw it away. Sure, another brilliant idea. Just like the brilliant idea that had him buying 20 percent of a New Jersey restaurant and putting up every penny he had in the world, and now the goddamn ocean was conspiring to bankrupt him by ruining the building. An act of God. Sometimes he thought God was just lying in wait, ready to ambush Trace on the road to happiness and prosperity.

He looked up and saw the big man coming toward the gate and again turned on the miniature tape recorder under his shirt.

"She said she'll see you," the man said. His tone of voice left no doubt about what he thought of *that* decision.

"Good. I thought she might."

He waited at the gate. The man waited on the other side. Finally, Trace said, "Well? Open the damn gate."

"She won't see you now," the man said.

"No? When?"

"This afternoon. She wants time to get herself together, I think she said."

"You mentioned the two million dollars?" Trace asked.

"I mentioned it."

"Usually, that gets me right in."

"I guess two million dollars doesn't mean as much to her as most. Go away. Come back at two o'clock."

"All right," Trace said. He started to turn from the gate, then asked, "What's your name?"

"Ferd. Why?"

"I wanted to be sure to ask for you when I come back," Trace said.

Trace drove around Westport looking for what appeared to be an honest saloon, then gave up the quest and went into a cocktail lounge in the center of town. He ordered Finlandia vodka on the rocks and tried to see past all the potted palms out through the main window at the business street in front. He had already decided he hated Westport. It was the kind of town where everything was neat and clean and polite and antiseptic and he thought he had seen more honest excitement, goodwill, and camaraderie in the eyes of a Las Vegas pit boss. There was an old map on the lounge's wall and Trace read off the Indian place-names. Indians, he thought. What the hell kind of Indians would have settled in Connecticut? Nondrinking Indians, no doubt. Indians had sold most of America for booze and beads. What had they gotten for Westport? Probably a divine quiche recipe. The Quiche Tribe.

He finished his drink quickly and ordered another. For months now, he realized, he had not really been drinking. Seventy-five percent of the time, for the past six months, he had been drinking wine. Seventy-five percent. And for what? To try to please a Japanese-Sicilian half-breed who was too mean and nasty and narrow-minded to lend him money, even to make herself rich.

And he had done it all, cutting the drinking, smoking less, even exercising every so often when he remembered, just to please Chico. Well, she didn't deserve it, and that was that.

He took a long vicious sip of his drink and looked at his watch. It wasn't two o'clock yet, not by a long sight. He had plenty of time left. He hated Westport. There weren't any real bars and the cocktail lounges didn't sell sausages or peanuts. For snacks, they didn't put out little cheesy fish-shaped crackers. Instead, they put out cereal bowls of crap made from whole grains. Sitting at a bar in Westport made him feel as if he should order a quart of milk so he could pour it over the snackies for breakfast.

He ordered another drink. And then he got change and bought cigarettes from the machine. Strong cigarettes. That'd fix her. He would show her. And he would never exercise again. He had done forty years quite nicely, thank you, without trying to "improve" himself to please her, and he was done being pussy-whipped. No more. Never again.

He thought about this through three more drinks and then, since it was two-thirty, decided it was time to return for his two-o'clock appointment with Mrs. Paddington. He felt good. He might even eat something later if he kept feeling this good.

Ferd was waiting for him when he parked near the Paddington gate.

"You're late," he said, sipping air.

"But I was early this morning," Trace said. "This makes up for it."

Ferd said nothing. He unlocked the gate, let Trace inside, then locked it again behind them. Wordlessly, he led Trace up the long paved driveway to the big sprawling house. Trace saw no animals and hoped that it was dogs' day off. How nice of Mrs. Paddington to arrange it on the day Trace visited. She might be a smart woman. Maybe she'd like to invest in a restaurant on the Jersey shore.

Trace sang as he walked:

Oh, the sons of the prophet
are hardy and bold and
quite unaccustomed to fear.
But the bravest by far
in the land of the shah,
was Abdul the Bulbul Emir.

The rest of it was about Ivan Skavinsky Skavar, but he couldn't remember the lyrics. Skavar rhymed with shah and czar and far, but Trace couldn't get the words together.

"Say, Ferd. Do you have a rhyming dictionary in the house?"

Ferd did not answer. Trace guessed that he didn't have a rhyming dictionary. Ivan Skavinsky Skavar would have to await another day.

As he got up the driveway, Trace could see that the red car in the driveway was a Saab station wagon. The gray one was the obligatory-for-Westport gray Mercedes sedan. This one had smoked windows in the rear.

Trace thought it was a particularly stupid idea to paint cars to look like battleships. Battleships were supposed to be gray so the enemy couldn't see them in the fog or mist, but what was the point of that with a car? If you owned a Mercedes, you wanted everybody to see it. That, he was sure, was the Westport rule.

And, come to think of it, it was a pretty stupid idea about battleships too. The fact was that navy vessels were painted gray way back when everything depended on visual sighting. But now the enemy had radar. Hell, even hanggliders had radar. So why not cheer up things? Paint navy war vessels in bright colors, pastels, pinks, reds, and purples. Mauve. Trace especially liked mauve. He bet that mauve ships would do a lot to boost the reenlistment rate in the navy. And it would strike terror in the hearts of the enemy to see the pride of the U.S. fleet come barrel-assing out of a fog bank, painted pink and purple and fuchsia and lime green.

He wondered if the navy paid for suggestions. Maybe he could get somebody who was in the navy to put the idea in the suggestion box and then split the reward with Trace. Sixty-forty. The sixty for Trace. He had to write the idea down someplace, but he never carried pencil or paper, so he turned on his tape recorder and said, "Think about repainting battleships."

"What?" Ferd said.

"Nothing. Just thinking aloud." He had it on tape now. He would never lose it.

He thought Ferd was going to take him through the garage like a tradesman, but at the last moment Ferd led him up the walk and in the front door of the house. A large wide stairway on the right led to the second floor.

"Mrs. Paddington's waiting for you in the drawing room. She's been waiting a long time," Ferd said.

"I'm worth waiting for," Trace said. He followed Ferd past the main stairway and down a dark hall. At the end of the hall, his foot bumped against something and he saw a folded wheelchair propped against the stairway wall.

He followed Ferd down a cross hall and into a large room. Even though the drapes had been pulled, the room was still quite bright. Mrs. Paddington sat on the sofa, her back to the main bank of windows. She smiled as the two men came in, and Trace knew he would recognize her anywhere by those teeth. He remembered a television commercial from his youth. It was for toothpaste and it showed a cartoon beaver and the jingle was "Bucky, Bucky Beaver, here's the new Ipana."

"Ferdinand," she said, "would you send Maggie in?"

"Sorry, Mrs. P. She's gone to market."

"Oh, I told her we'd want tea."

"It's made. She left it in the kitchen. I'll get it."

As Ferd left the room, Mrs. Paddington said, "Won't you sit down, Mr. Tracy?"

Trace remembered from her biography that the woman had been born in Hawaii of American parents, but she talked like Mrs. Colonel Blimp with a horsey haw-haw British accent.

"Chahmed, I'm sure," Trace said as he sat on a chair facing her across the coffee table.

He sat and forced himself to examine the woman. Her hair was a medium blond, but puffed up atop her head and sprayed so stiff that it looked like a wig that had been carved from a block of wood and then varnished.

Her features were regular and she might even have been attractive if it hadn't been for those top teeth jutting from her mouth like elephant tusks. Why hadn't she ever had dental work done? Tinted glasses hid her eyes from him.

"What can I do for you, Mr. Tracy?"

"I'm with the Garrison Fidelity Insurance Company."

"Yes, I saw that on your card." Her voice was deep and Trace finally nailed down the accent. She sounded like an upper-crust English-woman with no ear and no sense of humor trying to imitate Peter Sellers doing Inspector Clouseau. "Don't mind the glasses," she said.

"Something wrong?"

"A touch of conjunctivitis," she said.

"The old pinkeye," Trace said.

She nodded. Despite the heat, she was wear-ing a long robe over a long green-flowered nightgown. Her feet were encased in woolly slippers.

"I'm sorry to be bothering you," Trace said.

"It's no bother. Since I've been ill, I see so few people."

"It's about your husband and your insurance claim."

"Yes."

"This is just part of a routine check," Trace said. "We do it all the time."

"I don't know what I can tell you that I haven't told our lawyer. Have you spoken to him?"

"Not yet."

"I should have thought that would be your first stop." She sounded like a schoolmarm, Trace thought. He felt chastened, but before he could apologize, Ferd returned with a silver service that he placed on the table between them. He looked at Mrs. Paddington, who nodded and said, "That will be all."

"Call if you need me," he said.

"I will," she assured him.

When the door closed behind him, Trace said, "Very protective."

"I should say so. Ferdinand has been with my husband and me forever. Maggie, too."

She poured tea for the two of them without asking. Like all Brits, real or adopted, Mrs. Paddington just assumed that he would want tea as everyone she knew always wanted tea. But what Trace wanted was a drink. He didn't even drink tea in Chinese restaurants. It was a wonder the British ever had time to build an empire, with all their time spent with their noses in a teacup. Then, when they did drink, they drank gin. Gin belonged in bathtubs, not in people's stomachs. Trace gave up any hope that he was ever going to get anything worthwhile to drink in this house.

"I was wondering why you waited all these years to make your husband's death public," Trace said.

"I didn't really make it public," she said. "That happened after my counselor, Mr. Shapp, filed the court papers."

"Why so long after his disappearance?" Trace persisted.

"You didn't know Hemmie," she said as she handed him a teacup. She had nice hands, Trace thought. Smooth and soft, and he realized that she was only in her early forties. Her face belied it. Her skin seemed harsh and dry and wrinkled. That old devil sun.

"No, I didn't," Trace agreed.

"He is . . . was an exceptional man," she said. "When his plane vanished, I was sure that I would hear from him any day soon. I never really gave much thought to the possibility that he might be dead." She sipped at her tea. "Dead." She essayed the faintest of smiles, but even it exposed a lot of tooth and Trace wished she wouldn't smile. "I can say the word now. I wasn't able to for years. Dead."

"So you expected to hear from your husband one day," Trace said. "When did you realize you wouldn't?"

"I don't really know, Mr. Tracy. The time just went on, and each day was like the one before it and there was no Hemmie. You don't know what it's like, sitting alone, waiting, hoping and having that hope die a little every day."

"A couple of years, then," Trace said. "So you finally faced up to the fact that your husband wasn't coming home. Why didn't you report it to the authorities then?"

"What good would it have done? I was still clinging to a straw, Mr. Tracy. Maybe I still am, hoping that Hemmie might still turn up. And, well, to tell the truth, I didn't want to have to deal with anybody. I knew those press persons would be all over the place and I just wasn't really up to it. What difference does it make if the world knows Hemmie's dead or if it doesn't? He's still dead. What difference?"

"Two million dollars' difference to my company," Trace said.

"That was the last thing on my mind, Mr. Tracy. You know, if I were interested in the money, I wouldn't have had to wait seven years. Accidental deaths often do not require that wait, or so my attorney advises me. I just didn't want to deal with anyone. The truth is I have not been well since my husband's disappearance. I could not have handled disturbance of any kind."

"I can understand that," Trace said. "Is that why you moved from New Hampshire?"

"Yes. I thought I could be alone here."

"Is it wise to isolate yourself this way?" Trace said.

"Mr. Tracy, I am not beautiful, but neither

am I foolish enough to think I am. Why would I need people? I had the one man in my life who loved me and I lost him. Do you think I would ever find another like him? Or would I find a succession of money-hunting dandies who wanted to teach me the tango? I am quite happy being alone, Mr. Tracy." She looked at him for a few long seconds, replaced her teacup on the saucer, and said, "Perhaps not happy, sir, but being alone is certainly better than the alternatives I see available to me."

"So you came here."

"Yes. In West Hampstead—that was our home in New Hampshire—there were too many memories. Too many people who knew us. I will be content to see no one again."

"Except Ferdinand," Trace said.

"Yes. And Maggie. They have been with Hemmie and me since we returned from England. I hope they will stay with me until I die. Mr. Tracy, are you a detective or some such thing? Do you think this is some type of swindle and you are going to beat the truth out of me with a gun belt or whatever it is you people do?"

"No, I'm afraid not," Trace said. "My father's a private detective. That's more in his line. I'm a pacifist."

"Thank heavens. I was worried for a moment there."

"I have to ask you this question, Mrs. Paddington. Did your husband ever leave you for long stretches before?"

He saw her sit up straighter on the couch as if even her backbone were offended by the innuendo.

"Absolutely not," she snapped.

"And you have been a recluse since the accident?"

"The word 'recluse' is your choice, Mr. Tracy. I have just preferred to be alone. I haven't been well and . . . I spend most of my time in bed."

"Is that why you don't have any dogs here, Mrs. Paddington?" Trace asked. "That was a surprise to me."

"I can't take care of them, Mr. Tracy. I'm not well enough. And dogs are like people. They need love to thrive."

She lifted her teacup and seemed to try to hide behind it.

"Is there anything you can tell me about the accident?" Trace asked.

"Nothing that I haven't told the lawyer. Hemmie was a licensed pilot. He decided to join a protest against the killing of the harp seals in Newfoundland. We thought he'd beat the bad weather. So he kissed me good-bye and he left and I never saw him again," she said softly.

There was another soft sound in the room and it took Trace a moment to realize that Mrs. Paddington was sobbing.

He stood and mumbled, "I'll leave you now, Mrs. Paddington. Thank you for your time."

He went out into the hall, where he found Ferd.

"I think she needs you. She's a little upset," Trace said.

"I'll see you out first," Ferd said. "Then I'll tend to her."

The garage doors were open as they walked past.

"Nice cars," Trace said. Ferd said nothing.

"Nice day too," Trace tried, with the same result. So he reached under his jacket and turned off the tape recorder. No point in wasting good tape on somebody who didn't talk.

At the gate, Trace tried one last time. He said, "You know, I really feel sorry for Mrs. Paddington."

"Then don't bother her anymore," Ferd said, as he chained and locked the gate behind Trace.

5

Trace drove away from the house toward town, but a half-mile down the road, stopped, turned his car around, and went back and pulled into the driveway of the house just before Mrs. Paddington's.

The house was separated from the Paddington home by 125 feet of tall thick pines. Trace parked in the driveway and rang the front doorbell.

A woman opened the inside door. At least, Trace thought she was a woman. She was wearing a heavy jogging suit, despite the heat of the day, and she was so fat she looked like a repulsive mound of laundry. Across the front of her sweatshirt was lettered: FREE HINCKLEY. The person was wearing a wool knit cap pulled down over her ears, wristbands, and ankle-high army green sneakers. She was holding Heavyhands weights, and as she looked at Trace, she jogged up and down in place.

"Yes?" she said through the screen door. Her voice was clearly that of a woman.

"Is the man of the house in?" Trace asked.

"Tacky," she puffed. "Very tacky."

"Why tacky?" Trace asked.

"These are the 1980s, mister. You don't go around anymore asking for 'the man of the house.' Anything you've got to say nowadays, you can say to either of us. We are equal."

"Ooops, sorry," Trace said.

"So what did you want?"

"I'm taking orders on vasectomies," Trace mumbled.

"What?" the woman asked. Jog, jog, jog, jump, jump, jump.

Trace spoke up. "I'm from the Garrison Fidelity Insurance Company." He held up a business card and the woman perused it through the screen door. Trace wondered if it was hard to read while jogging up and down in place, while pumping Heavyhands over your head at the same time. If you could read while running, why not a reading collar for runners? Like those things that Bob Dylan used to wear to make believe he could play the harmonica while he was making believe he could sing and play the guitar. Runners could jog and still keep up with their reading. They could study the latest medical statistics on fatal coronaries suffered while jogging. It might be a big-hit item and Trace told himself to remember to make a note of it. Someday, when he retired rich from the restaurant business, he might want to have that one patented. If the people next door could make a fortune out of dog doo, then he should be able to make a dynasty out of a read-while-running device.

"Okay," the woman said. "I see the card. What would you like?" She was still jogging in place. Just then, a giant hound skidded around the corner behind her, into view. It was an enormous shepherd that Trace thought might have a career shot at herding elephants. He growled savagely at Trace.

"Nice dog," Trace said. "Pretty bowwow."

The dog took a step closer to the screen door and snarled and salivated.

Great, Trace thought, caught between a distrustful fat feminist and a maniacal hound.

"Let me make one thing perfectly clear," Trace said. "I'm not trying to sell you insurance. Make no mistake about that." He considered doing his Richard Nixon impersonation but decided not to. The last time he did, someone thought he was imitating W. C. Fields and he was weeks recovering his sense of self.

"Hoho," the woman said, still running in place.

"Why hoho?"

"The last person who came to the door and said he wasn't selling anything wound up filling my basement with a worthless freezer and sides of beef. What do you do with a side of beef?" She jogged; the dog snarled.

"Rocky punched them and look where he wound up," Trace said.

"Who's Rocky?"

"You know. Sylvester Stallone, mumbles, moom pitchers, Marlon Brando impersonations?"

"I don't like Sylvester Stallone," the woman said.

"I think he is the quintessential classical actor of our time. He has cut away all the frills and reduced acting to its basic core essential."

"What basic essential?" she asked.

"Showing up on the set on time and sober," Trace said. "A great contribution to filmatic theory."

She was still jogging up and down. Trace liked to look people in the eyes when he talked to them, but it was hard when the eyes kept moving. He wondered if she would be offended if he jogged up and down on the top step, in time with her. Then he decided that Baskerville, the dog, might disapprove even if she didn't. He held his ground.

"Okay," she said, and puffed out. "Sell me what you're not going to sell me."

"Really, I'm not a salesman. I'm doing a survey on life insurance among the upper classes of America."

"That's us. What do you want to know?"

"Do you or your husband carry life insurance?"

"I wouldn't know, puff, puff. You'd have to talk to my husband."

"And the man of the house isn't home?" Trace said.

"No man of the house is home. This is Westport, Mr. Salesman."

"Westport," Trace said. "That's right. Westport, La Jolla, and Grosse Pointe. That's my survey territory."

"Every man in Westport works in New York City. They're all gone till seven-thirty tonight. Some until Friday night 'cause they stay in town all week."

"I see. And you don't know about your life insurance."

"Not a thing," she said.

Trace nodded in the direction of Mrs. Paddington's home. The dog growled and moved a few inches closer to the screen.

"How about the folks next door?" he said. "Think they might be helpful?"

"I don't think you can get in to find out," she said. Jog, jog, jog, pump, pump, pump. Trace was getting sweaty watching her.

"How's that?" he asked.

"Well, first of all, the husband's dead," she said.

"Sorry to hear that," Trace said.

" 'S all right. He died a long time ago. But they don't see anybody."

"Who's they?"

"There's a woman living there, the widow, and she's got a couple of servants, but you can't get in."

"Maybe you could get her to see me? I mean, give her a call, you know, a neighbor and ask her to talk to me. I'd appreciate it," Trace said.

"You don't understand. They don't see anybody. Not even me."

"You're the next-door neighbor and you're not friends?" Trace said.

"Friends? I've never even been in the house."

Trace was silent. As so often happened, the woman got nervous with the silence and kept talking.

"They moved here a few years ago and I baked them a garbanzo loaf, sort of like a welcome cake, and I brought it over there."

"And?" Trace said.

"The guard took it at the gate and said that Mrs. Paddington, that's their name, wasn't well and not seeing anybody but that he would see she got the loaf. He didn't even let me through the gate."

"Then what happened?"

"Nothing," she said. "No phone call, no thank you, and I even put my name on the side of the loaf pan with my phone number so she could call but she didn't."

"That's not very neighborly," Trace said.

Her eyes were still going up and down as she

jogged in place. "Try this," she puffed. "About a week later, I came out of the house one day and the loaf pan was right there on top of the milk box."

"At least you got your pan back," Trace said.

"Yeah. But the garbanzo loaf was still in it. It wasn't even touched. Is that rude or what?"

"Rude, definitely rude. Garbanzos have feelings too. So that's it?"

"Sum and substance of all my dealings with my next-door neighbors."

"You don't see them in church or at the market or anything?" Trace asked.

"Once in a while I see the maid at the supermarket."

"Is she nice?"

"I don't even know her name. We don't talk," the woman said.

"I guess there's not much point in my trying to talk to those folks, then, is there?" Trace asked.

"You wouldn't get past the gate."

"I want to thank you for taking this time out of your busy day. You've been very helpful to me."

"I didn't tell you anything," the woman said.

"But you tried, and in this world of woe and tragedy, good intentions count for a lot."

"I'd rather have the money. Listen, talk to the woman across the street. She's nosy and she might know something."

"Thank you. It's been nice talking to you through the door this way. Would it help if I stayed and counted cadence for you?"

As he walked back to his car, Trace told himself that it wasn't really a wasted stop. After all, he had come up with the good idea of a reading gadget for joggers. And all a man needed to become wealthy, really wealthy, was one good idea. That, and a little investment capital. As soon as the restaurant opened and started producing money, Trace would have no shortage of investment capital. The future looked bright. *If* the restaurant ever opened . . .

Trace backed out into the street and drove up the roadway to the house directly across the street from Mrs. Paddington's. He parked in front of the closed garage door, walked to the front entrance, and rang the bell.

"No one's there," a woman's voice called out.

Trace looked around but saw no one.

"Over here," the voice called. "Behind the big tree."

On the far side of a big pine tree, Trace found a woman lying on a towel on the neatly clipped lawn. She was wearing the skimpiest of two-piece bathing suits; her hair was fire-red and shiny, her skin very tan. Her eyes were large and jade-green. She had turned on her side to await Trace, with her head propped on one hand. The curve of her hip nipping into a small waist as she lay there was like the female curve in a sketch of Picasso's—simple, yet totally womanly. Her bosom was very large.

"Are you the lady of the house?" Trace asked.

"I hope I don't look like the man of the house?" the woman said. She smiled. Her teeth were large and even and very white, her lips wide and full and seemingly dark red without the use of lipstick. Her eyelashes were so thick that they looked as if they had been baked in a kiln, but she wore no other makeup and Trace thought that perhaps the lashes were just another of nature's gifts to her.

Next to her, a glass was held in a coiled metal ring, attached to a metal rod stuck into the ground. A lawn drink holder. Trace was impressed and wished he had invented that. Another glass, empty, was in a holder next to hers.

"No," Trace said. "No mistaking you for the man of the house. You live here, I take it?"

The woman rolled onto her back and smiled at Trace, who, standing there, suddenly understood the meaning of jumping one's bones. He kept himself vertical by an act of will.

"Before you get all involved in business discussions and boring stuff, would you like a drink?" she asked.

"Yes. My lips are suddenly dry."

"Pour yourself one." She handed him a glass pitcher that had been under the tree.

"What is it?"

"Westport Windjammers," she said. "Vodka and tequila and rum and whatever fruit juice you can find around the house."

"What kind did you find?" Trace asked.

"Lime Kool-Aid was all I could find."

"Good. Just the way I like it." He poured a glass, drank half of it, refilled his glass, put it in the lawn glass holder, marveled at its construction, the low cost of the item, imagined the profit he could make with a six-to-one markup over manufacturing cost, then sat on the towel where the woman was patting a place next to her.

"Should I do business now?" Trace said.

"If you must."

"Your husband's not home, I take it?"

"Does it matter to you?"

"Not unless he's bigger than me," Trace said.

"He's not."

"Good. I'm from the Garrison Fidelity Insurance Company."

"Oh, God. You're not going to try to sell me insurance, are you?"

"Of course not, Mrs.—Mrs.—?"

"Patrick. Mrs. Patrick. But you can call me Elvira."

"It's a pretty name," Trace said.

"Thank you," she said. "I feel like an Elvira today."

"I feel like an Elvira today too," Trace said. "Anyway, I'm not selling insurance. I'm doing a survey."

"I thought they hired college kids to do that kind of stuff, you know, house to house, asking insipid questions."

"Don't send a boy to do a man's job," Trace said.

"I'll remember you said that. What's your name?"

"Devlin Tracy. My friends call me Trace."

"And what do your enemies call you?" she asked.

"I only have three. One of them calls me her ex-husband. The other two call me Daddy."

"You sound as if you've had a tough life," she said. Her breasts were really wonderful, Trace decided as she snaked a long thin arm over to take her drink from its holder.

"Not so tough. Anyway, about the insurance. Probably you can't answer these questions. Maybe your husband might know more about it."

"My husband's in New York and won't be back until Friday night."

"How does he stand being away from you?"

"He has a mistress. He stays with her Monday through Thursday. I get him Friday, Saturday, and Sunday."

"That doesn't bother you?"

"Only on Monday through Thursday. I hate to sleep alone."

"I mean, his having a mistress," Trace said.

"No, we can afford it and she's a nice girl."

"You've met her?"

"We have lunch together when I go to New York. Bart is working, so we have lunch. After all, we've got a lot in common."

"If that's true, Bart's the luckiest man in the world," Trace said as he finished his drink and poured a refill. It was a very large pitcher.

"It's true enough. She's very beautiful. Bart has a good eye. So what questions did you want to ask?"

"I'm wondering about the life-insurance levels that you and your husband maintain," Trace said, trying to sound very businesslike.

"Does that mean how much insurance do we have?"

"Right. Insurance."

"All right. Bart's got a hundred-thousand-dollar policy for each of his first three wives as beneficiaries. That's three hundred thousand dollars. And he's got five hundred thousand dollars with me as beneficiary. So that's eight hundred thousand dollars."

"What about you, Elvira?"

"I don't have any insurance."

"Shouldn't you have?"

"No. I can't think of a reason why I should."

"Neither can I," Trace said. "I think life insurance is a rip-off."

"Not all of it. If Bart dies, I'll need it to maintain this house. To keep the pitcher full, so to speak."

"Good thinking. You're a very bright woman."

"Bright and fortunate," she said. "My cup runneth over."

"All of them," Trace said, glancing down at her bosom. Then he glanced down the long flow of grass rolling away toward the road. He could see the Paddington gates and home across the street.

"Are those all your questions?" Elvira asked.

"That's all I needed to know," Trace said. "How about those people who live over there?" He pointed toward the Paddington house.

"What about them?"

"Do you think they'll help me with my survey?"

"You tell me. What kind of answers did they give you when you were there before?"

"Oh, you saw me," he said.

"I remembered the car. You don't see many dark-blue cars anymore. What did they tell you?"

"Nothing, really. Mr. Paddington is dead and they have a million-dollar insurance policy and they're trying to collect on it. I was just wondering what kind of people they are."

"You're not really doing a survey, are you?" Elvira asked.

"No," Trace said, surprised at his own outburst of honesty. "I'm checking their insurance claim."

"Are you a detective? God, are you going to rip my clothes off and shove a gat into my belly unless I come clean?"

"More like an investigator," Trace said. "Hold the gat idea." He sipped at his drink and saw she was smiling at him. "You know anything that might be helpful? About your neighbors?"

"I don't know. Aren't you private eyes supposed to pay your stoolies for important information?"

"It's usually negotiable," Trace said.

"Then negotiate."

"How about dinner tonight?" Trace said.

"That'll do for a start," she said. "I've never seen Mrs. Paddington. I read about her in the newspapers a few weeks ago, how her husband died and she was having him declared dead. That's all I know. The woman who works there is named Maggie Winters, I think. Did you meet her?"

"No," Trace said.

"Oh. Well, she's pretty if you like the blond peasant sort. The only other person I see there is the big gorilla. The one you were talking to earlier today."

"You've been here all day?" Trace asked.

"All day, every day. At least during the summer. I see all and know all," Elvira said.

"But you don't know anything about the Paddingtons?"

"Nothing. And I know the gossip about everybody."

"How do you do that if you're always on the lawn?" Trace asked.

"Well, not literally always. I have to go to the hairdresser and the weekly facial and aerobics classes, so I get out a bit. But nobody knows anything about the Paddingtons."

"I wish I could find somebody who did. You know what they do for a living?" Trace said.

"Something to do with dog shit, the newspaper said."

"Not in so many words," Trace said.

"Not exactly, but the meaning was clear. Anyway, you can tell me all about it at dinner."

"Sounds good," Trace said.

"And I'll see if I can find out anything about the Paddingtons."

"That sounds good too," Trace said.

"Are you staying in town?"

"Ye Olde English Motel."

"What a dump," Elvira said. "What room?"

"Three-seventeen."

"I'll call you at seven-thirty tonight and pick you up," she said.

"I could pick you up," Trace said.

"No. Somebody might see us and besides . . ."

"Besides what?"

"I wouldn't want anybody I know to see me in a dark-blue Ford."

6

At least Trace approved of the caliber of women in Westport, he thought as he waited in Adam Shapp's law office, pretending to read a magazine and watching the lawyer's receptionist.

She was barely out of her teens and her skin seemed to sparkle. Probably in an effort to look more mature, her hair was pulled back tightly from her forehead and tied up in a bun and she wore large praying-mantis-like eyeglasses. But if the impression she wanted to give was one of all business, it hadn't worked because she reminded Trace of one of those before-and-after scenes from a thirties' movie where the librarian, prim and proper by day, rips off her glasses, lets down her hair, and at night stomps the stage at Minsky's, bumping and grinding to the tune of "Let's Do It in the Road."

It wasn't just Westport either. All towns with a lot of money seemed to have more than their share of good-looking women. Was that cause or effect? Trace wondered. Did beautiful women naturally tend to towns where people were wealthy? That was cause. Or did women in rich towns have more time to spend making themselves and their children beautiful? That was effect.

No way of knowing, Trace decided. That was the way life was. You passed through it and there were a lot of things that you wondered about and were never able to get answers to. Like why store clerks with acne were always rude. Why Alka-Seltzer fizzed when it got wet. How anyone ever learned to speak German. You left the world as dumb as when you arrived. The only difference was that you wore clothes when leaving.

He looked away from the receptionist and took up a back copy of a psychology magazine. It flipped open to a page in which a postcard had been inserted, soliciting readers' answers to a survey. Trace read the survey question:

"If you were the President of the United States and the U.S. was losing a war and the only way you could avert defeat was to launch a nuclear strike, knowing that such a strike would prompt a retaliatory response, would you use nuclear weapons?"

What a stupid question, Trace thought. What

kind of war was the U.S. losing? What would happen to the U.S. if it lost the war? How could you make a decision without knowing the answers to those questions?

He got up and took a pen from a wooden cup on the receptionist's desk and came back to fill in the card.

He marked the box that read, "Yes, I would use nuclear weapons." Beneath it was a space for "Explain your actions."

"Because I like to kill people," Trace wrote.

He thought about it for a while, then filled in the name of Michiko Mangini and their address in Las Vegas. Maybe they would send someone to interview her and annoy her. That would serve her right.

Suppose they sent her a free subscription for having the best answer? If they did, he'd make sure the subscription was transferred to him. He'd start watching the mail just to be sure. He hadn't been paying enough attention to the mail lately.

"Mr. Tracy."

Trace looked up and the receptionist said, "Mr. Shapp will see you now." Trace nodded, put down the magazine, but stuck the postcard in his pocket. He walked toward the heavy mahogany door in the rear of the office.

"Mr. Tracy?" the receptionist said again.

"Yes?"

"The pen, please?"

"Oh. Heh, heh." He took the ballpoint pen from his jacket pocket and handed it back to her. "Just forgot, I guess."

"I'm glad I remembered for the two of us," she said.

Snotty little twerp, he thought. Thinking that he would try to steal a cheap ballpoint pen.

Adam Shapp was younger than Trace had expected. The tall blond man who hadn't seen thirty yet was standing at his bank of office windows, looking out over the Post Road. As he turned, Trace saw he was wearing a three-piece gray suit with a Phi Beta Kappa key hanging from the vest. He was tan and his light-blond hair was trimmed neatly and he had light ice-blue eyes. He looked as if he should be playing at Wimbledon, not hanging around a law office.

He smiled as he stepped forward to shake Trace's hand. He was almost as tall as Trace and looked to be in a lot better shape. He was probably rich too, Trace thought. Young and rich and tan and smart and handsome. The boy from Ipanema. Hell, he probably had inherited a bank in Ipanema. He probably never had had to raise ten thousand dollars in a hurry to keep a restaurant deal alive to secure his future. Trace had a powerful urge to punch him, even while the lawyer's hand was extended in friendship. Aaaah, he was probably a black-belt karate expert too and Trace would wind up getting his ass kicked. He settled for shaking his hand.

"How are you, Mr. Tracy?" the young man said. "Please sit down."

Trace plopped into a chair facing the attorney's desk.

"Would you like a cup of coffee?"

"No."

"Something else?"

"What does something else consist of?" Trace asked.

"Tea. Herbal tea. Bouillon. Maybe we've got some diet Coke."

"I've always regarded my body as a temple, Mr. Shapp. I wouldn't put any of that junk in it."

The lawyer nodded and pressed the intercom button. "Sandy. Black coffee, please. Yes, just one."

He arranged Trace's business card neatly in the center of his desk blotter, looked at it again, then up at Trace. "I expect you're here to talk about Mrs. Paddington and her petition to the courts?"

Trace nodded.

"We've got a court date in . . . let's see." Shapp opened a red leather-covered date book and skimmed through the pages. "In three weeks. Mr. Paddington will be legally declared dead then. So what can I do for you?"

"I'm looking into Mr. Paddington's disappearance."

"You too? Your company had detectives doing

that for a couple of weeks. Didn't they find out enough?"

"I guess not," Trace said. "Anyway, I'm like the last big gun they like to fire before they give up. Hope to frighten away the enemy troops. And if they don't run, then we surrender."

"It's really kind of annoying, you know," Shapp said as he sat down. "The case is very simple and you would think your company would stop fooling around and start writing the check."

"They hate to part with money," Trace said. "It's all Walters Marks' fault."

"Who's Walter Marks?" Shapp asked.

"He's the vice-president for claims. He thinks that anybody who carries more than a thousand dollars' insurance only took out the policy to defraud old Gone Fishing."

"Gone Fishing? Oh, Garrison Fidelity. Okay. Remind me never to buy any insurance from Walter Marks."

"I'll send you a note every couple of months," Trace promised.

Sandy, the receptionist, came in, carrying a cup of coffee, in a real cup, on a real saucer, on a wooden tray. She put it down squarely atop Trace's business card.

"Thanks, Sandy," Shapp said.

"Keep your eye on your pens, Mr. Shapp," she said, and smiled toward Trace as she walked out.

"What did that mean?" Shapp asked him.

"She caught me trying to lift one of her pens," Trace said. "I didn't know it was such a matter of pride with her."

"You're lucky you didn't go after the paper clips. The cops would have been called," the young lawyer said. He sipped at his coffee and looked at Trace as if inviting a question.

"Will Mrs. Paddington be able to testify at the hearing?" Trace asked.

"If it's necessary, I imagine so. It probably won't be."

"I got the impression she was pretty much of an invalid."

"You talked to her?"

"This afternoon," Trace said.

"Well, she's obviously not in the best of health. But if your company wastes our time and she has to go to court, she's got those two people to bring her."

"Ferdinand and Maggie?" Trace said.

"Right. The loyal retainers," Shapp said.

"What do you think of Mrs. Paddington?" Trace asked.

"She's an arsonist, a cold-blooded murderer, and a pathological liar," Shapp said. "Come on, Tracy. She's my client. What the hell am I supposed to think about her? She's a poor woman with a dead husband and she wants her insurance money. She'll probably spend it all on cat food or something. Do I think she's playing with a full deck? I don't know, the allure of animals hasn't ever reached me. But this is all cut and dried, so I'm going to do my job, take my fee, and be done with it."

"Me too," Trace said. "How'd Mrs. Paddington happen to retain you?"

"Yellow Pages, I guess. I didn't ask. I hardly ever reject clients because they don't come with letters of introduction."

"You think this is just going to breeze through court, don't you?" Trace asked.

"It's just a formality. It's done every day. The only thing that makes this different is your company's going to have to cough up two million dollars. Insurance companies ought to pay. That's what they're in business for."

"You tell that to Mrs. Paddington?"

"Sure."

"You talk to her a lot?" Trace asked.

"Not much. Once in a while on the phone. She types me little notes when she wants to remind me of something. I wouldn't call us real close."

"How about Mr. Paddington? What do you know about him?"

"Nothing except that he's dead," Shapp said. "What'd he do, make his money in pooper-scoopers or something, right? And then from Mrs. Paddington, I get that he was harmless enough. Big in save the animals. His plane goes down when, what, what's he trying to do, save the harp seal or the woolly mastodon or whatever it is? What do I know about him? That's about it."

"Not an animal lover? It's hard to believe," Trace said.

"Hey, just because I live in this sappy town, don't think I buy all this trendy crap. Save the seals, natural childbirth, bean sprouts, tofu, raw fish, it's all bullshit."

"You don't think there's a chance that Paddington's hiding out somewhere?" Trace asked.

"You've been reading too many detective novels, Mr. Tracy. First of all, the Paddingtons are wealthy. I don't think they've been spending the last seven years trying to figure out how to rip off What-his-name?"

"Walter Marks. Write it down. Send him a nasty note," Trace suggested.

"Yeah. Walter Marks. They don't need the hassle or the money."

"Do you know who Mrs. Paddington's doctor is?" Trace asked.

"No. It never came up. Why?"

"I don't know," Trace said honestly. "Maybe somebody'll tell me this is the tenth husband she's buried. Something like that."

"Good luck," Shapp said. "I don't think so."

"Do you think the Paddingtons got along?" Trace asked.

"I never met him, but she thinks he was a

saint. I'm surprised she didn't build a shrine to him in the yard. Anything else?"

"How do you stay so thin?" Trace asked.

"Being young. I'll worry about middle-aged spread in middle age."

As Trace got up, Shapp asked, "What do you do now?"

"I don't know," Trace said. "I'm going to have to hang around 'cause I need to justify my existence. Unless you've got ten thousand dollars you want to lend me."

"I don't think so. Are you going to make ten thousand dollars just for looking around?"

"Only if I find something."

"You're out of luck, then. What do you need the ten thousand for? Or is it personal?"

"I own a piece of this restaurant at the Jersey shore. It suffered some storm damage and I've got to come up with repair money. You interested? I could make you a good deal."

"Not me. I don't trust restaurants. Did you know that seventy-five percent of all restaurants fail?"

"Is everybody I meet subscribing to the same clipping service? I can't turn around without somebody telling me that my restaurant's going to go belly-up."

"Sorry. Those are the brutal facts," Shapp said.

"I'm staying in the deal," Trace said stubbornly.

"If you need a good lawyer to get you out of the deal, keep me in mind," Shapp said.

Sandy was not at the reception desk when Trace left. He stole all the ballpoint pens from the penholder.

7

"Hello, Ed. How's the storm damage?"

"Still damaged. Where's the fourteen thousand dollars?"

"Hold, hold, hold, and hold," Trace said. "Fourteen thousand?"

"Your share of the repairs."

"Holy Mary, Mother of Gawd," Trace said. "I talked to you a couple of days ago and it was ten thousand dollars."

"It was ten, maybe twelve. Now it's fourteen. We just got estimates on the work that's got to be done before we can open."

"Get new estimates," Trace said. "Better yet, it's fucking water damage, isn't it?"

"Yes," Ed said.

"Then buy a bunch of mops, hire a bunch of college kids. Don't pay them more than three bucks an hour. Have them mop up the water. Buy two sunlamps to dry the place out. It shouldn't cost but two hundred dollars and I'll have my forty bucks in the mail to you tomorrow."

"Very funny," Ed said.

"Did you hear anybody chuckling on this end?" Trace said. "What the hell can a storm damage? The building didn't fall down, did it?"

"No."

"Good. Then mop and dry it."

"You can't mop and dry a ruined electrical system. A burned-out boiler. An air-conditioner that's got to be rebuilt. A monitoring system for the bar that's got water in the lines. Your share's fourteen thousand dollars."

"What the hell kind of investment is this?" Trace demanded. "You said this was going to be something for my old age. A steady regular income that would last me the rest of my life, and now the freaking place isn't even open yet and it's already driving me to the poorhouse."

"Sorry, Trace, but we've got to get these repairs done to get our certificate of occupancy. You can't open a restaurant without one. As soon as we're open, the money'll come pouring in."

"You're a pain in my ass," Trace said. "I want out. You want to buy me out?"

"I don't have the money right now," Ed said.

"How about one of the other partners? Hell,

they're all going to get rich, right? Tell them buy me out and they'll get twice as rich."

"No interest there."

"How do you know that?" Trace asked suspiciously. "How do you know nobody wants to buy me out when I just asked you this very minute?"

"I have a sense of what the other partners think."

"How'd you get such a well-developed sense of what other people think?" Trace said.

"Actually, I've checked with the other partners. Just in case."

"You son of a bitch, you're trying to sell out your own shares, aren't you?" Trace shouted into the telephone.

"Calm down. Aren't we friends?"

"I thought we were until this, you goddamn pirate," Trace said.

"I was just trying to gauge what our other partners were thinking," Ed said.

"Gauge this," Trace said. "You're not getting any fourteen thousand from me. Not a penny more than ten thousand."

"When can I have it?"

"Hold it. My share's fourteen, but I offer you ten and you're willing to take it? What the hell kind of estimate was it you got for repairs anyway? You're a thief."

"If I get ten from you, I can pay the repair people a partial payment. Maybe I can hold them off for the rest until the place opens," Ed said.

"Maybe they'll take the fee in free dinners and do the job for no cash," Trace said.

"I'm hurt, Trace," the other man said. "I bet you think that this is easy for me."

"Easy or hard, I don't care. But I never thought it was real hard to waste other people's money. Christ, the Third World does it all the time."

"I need at least ten thousand dollars' good-faith money from you. When can I have it?"

"What happens if you don't get it?" Trace asked.

"We renege on our notes. We never open. The bank forecloses. They sell the place at auction."

"Cut the crap. What really happens?"

"You get back maybe a dime on a dollar on the money you already put in. When can I have the ten-thousand-dollar down payment?"

"I'm working on it," Trace said.

"Work real fast. I need it right away. I'd hate to see you go down on this deal. Particularly when just a few more dollars and it's all broad sunlit highways for the rest of our lives."

"Yeah, rolling right to the poorhouse gates," Trace growled as he slammed down the telephone.

Trace lit another cigarette even though he had one burning in the ashtray. The maid had removed his butt can and he went into the bathroom, poured water again into the bottom of the wastepaper basket, brought it outside, and set it next to the bed. He stubbed out both cigarettes burning in the ashtray, dumped their remains into the butt can, and lit another cigarette.

Being an entrepreneur was a lousy way to try to make a living, he thought. All his good ideas—and there were a lot of them—always required a lot of start-up money and he never had enough. He had never had any money when he was an accountant, and now that he worked for Garrison Fidelity, he didn't have any more.

Only once had anything good ever happened in his life. He had come into some money on a real-estate deal and used the proceeds to buy his way out of his marriage. He left his wife and two children and had gone to Las Vegas to be a professional gambler.

Just about the time he was tired of gambling for a living, he had met Bob Swenson, the president of Garrison Fidelity Insurance. Swenson had been clipped of a million dollars in negotiable securities by a hooker and Trace had arranged to get the securities back. In gratitude, Swenson had put Trace on retainer as an occasional investigator for Garrison Fidelity.

About the same time, he met Chico. He had found her, naked, in an apartment-building hallway, after some man had gotten her liquored up, then thought it was cute to throw her out into the hall without clothes.

Trace got her clothes back, punched the man's lights out, and then helped her find a job as a blackjack dealer at the Araby Casino. The idea of supplementing her income by turning occasional tricks for out-of-town gamblers was hers alone. He had never been able to ask her why.

He smoked some more and thought about Garrison Fidelity and realized he was tired of working, scratching around trying to make a living. The restaurant deal was supposed to end all that and free his time so he could devote it to other money-making ideas.

He thought it was unfair. He was one of the world's great natural resources, a money-making machine ready to be unleashed. But he was never going to get a chance unless he came up with another ten thousand dollars.

How to get it?

Of course. There was a way. A simple way.

He would beg for it.

He called Chico in their Las Vegas condominium.

"Hello, light of my life," he said when she answered the phone.

"I'm still not lending you any money," she said by way of greeting.

"Did I even ask you for any?"

"Not yet in this phone conversation. That out of the way, how goes it?"

"It doesn't go. So far, this is a dead end. Don't change the subject so fast. Let's talk about lending me money."

"Let's not," Chico said.

"Why not?"

"Because it'll vanish, poof, up in smoke. I've been with you for how long?"

"Four years. It only seems longer," Trace said.

"Four years. I've heard every one of your lunatic ideas. Make Tulsa into a parking lot. Backward printed signs for cars, combination combs and toothbrushes for muff divers—"

"Just a minute. I never invented any such thing," he said.

"Then I must just have. It's yours, free. Take it and run with it, Trace. Just don't ask me to invest."

"I'm not asking you to invest in this restaurant, Chico."

"Good."

"I'm begging you. I'm here in this awful town, down on both knees, begging you. Save me. You're all that stands between me and a life of destitution."

"No."

"Didn't I quit smoking for you?" he asked.

"For three hours once. You're back up to four packs a day."

"If I knew it meant that much to you. I would have stayed stopped. I'll quit again as soon as I get back," Trace promised.

"I don't believe you."

"And didn't I quit drinking?"

"No. You quit drinking vodka. Some of the

time. Instead of drinking a quart of vodka a day, now you drink a gallon of wine. Maybe a gallon and a half when you're going good. All I got out of that big change is that the garbage is heavier now when I have to carry it to the incinerator."

"I'll stop drinking and smoking as soon as I get back. I'll even start carrying out the garbage."

"Don't do it for me. I won't lend you ten thousand dollars."

"Fourteen thousand," Trace said.

"Ho, ho, ho. Maybe you can make that much money writing jokes for Rodney Dangerfield," Chico said.

"You're an ungrateful wretch," Trace said.

"Maybe, but I've got to watch out for myself," she said.

"I'm going to keep drinking and smoking," he said.

"Suit yourself. Since you're going to be poor, you might as well be dead."

"And women," he said.

"What about women?"

"I have been straight for the longest time now," Trace said.

"You have never been straight."

"If I've got the name, I might as well have the game. I'm going back to seeing other women."

"As opposed to?"

"In fact, I've got a date tonight. With a beautiful redhead," Trace said.

"Wonderful," Chico said. "I've got a date too. If we pick someplace between Connecticut and Nevada, maybe all four of us can meet for dinner."

"You're not going to help me, are you? In this moment of need?" Trace said. "That's what you're hinting at, isn't it?"

"Now you're catching on," Chico said. "If you need the money so badly, do a good job on this case. Earn it. The old-fashioned way."

"Anybody can earn money," Trace said. "I want to beg for it."

"Well, beggars can be losers," Chico said.

"You know, you're free, piebald, and twenty-one. You can turn me down if you want."

"I want," Chico said.

"I'll never forgive you."

"I'll try to endure," she said.

"I've got to dress for dinner," Trace said. "With the redhead."

"That's odd. I've got to undress for dinner," Chico said.

"Don't go doing anything dirty in my bed," he yelled, but the telephone went dead in his ear.

She probably wasn't going to lend him the money, Trace decided as he replaced the telephone. He smoked some more and killed the bottle of vodka. He thought some more about his resources. This didn't take much time because his resources were nil.

All the money he had in the world was tied up in the restaurant at Oceanbright. He had no other savings and he didn't know anyone who would lend him money. Bob Swenson had consistently refused to lend him a dime. Walter Marks was out. He would only laugh if Trace asked him for money. There was his father, Sarge.

But Sarge wouldn't have it. He had his pension from the New York City Police Department, but any secret savings he might have had would have gone to open up his private-detective agency. And even if Sarge had had money, it would all be in joint accounts with Trace's mother. Hilda Tracy was not ready to lend her son anything except good advice, like Be Thrifty, Don't Get in Over Your Head, and Walk Before You Run, and a million other stupid homilies all orated in capital letters.

Who else did he know who had money?

There was his ex-wife. She might have some. But to borrow money from her, he would have to talk to her and that violated an oath he had made the day they were divorced. His two children, What's-his-name and the girl, didn't have any money. At least he didn't think they did. They were still little. How old were they? They were something and something. What's-his-name was older. Maybe.

Trace wished he believed in telepathy. He could send his ex-wife a message to lend him money. Ten thousand dollars, fourteen if she had it. He closed his eyes and concentrated, forming words slowly and distinctly inside his brain.

"Cora. Are you listening? Please listen, Cora. I'm in the Ye Olde—that's with an 'e'—English Motel in Westport, Connecticut, and I am in dire need of . . . say, fifteen thousand dollars. Fifteen thousand, Cora. You got that? Call me now at the Ye Olde English Motel in Westport, Connecticut. Offer me the loan of fifteen thousand dollars. Are you listening? Hurry. My life depends on it."

He stopped concentrating and lay on the bed with his eyes closed, trying to be a receptacle for return messages. Nothing came in.

The telephone didn't ring either.

He looked around the room and saw his suitcase in the corner. Maybe he would unpack his clothing. Then he saw the vodka bottle was empty. He would unpack his clothing later.

He hooked up the microphone tie clip for his tape recorder. The microphone was a golden frog with an open mouth. Mesh that covered the mouth concealed the small microphone.

As he left the room, he yelled at the telephone, "Cora, you were always a cheap bitch."

8

Richie, the bartender at the motel cocktail lounge, remembered Trace from the night before.

"You were really flying last night," he said. "Did you get your ten thousand dollars?"

"Fourteen," Trace said. "No. You want to lend it to me?"

"I'll make you a drink," Richie said. He filled an old-fashioned glass with Finlandia, dropped in two ice cubes, and set it on the bar in front of Trace.

"If I had the money, maybe I'd like to get into a restaurant deal," the bartender said. "But you need a banker. I'm just a bartender."

"Don't say it like that," Trace said. "Bartenders are real important."

"Somebody's got to mix the drinks, right?"

"No," Trace said. "Bartenders contribute a lot in a lot of ways. Literature, for instance."

"Run that one by me again," Richie said. He was a tall young man with a pleasant face and he looked slightly ill-at-ease wearing the leather tunic that Ye Olde English Motel inflicted on its service employees.

"Dickens, for instance," Trace said. "Do you know that a bartender was responsible for Dickens' success?"

"I didn't know that. How?"

"Dickens was a drinker, a real heavy-duty boozer," Trace said. "One day, he was stuck on a book, so he walked over to his favorite pub and he asked the bartender to make him a martini."

"Did they have martinis then?" Richie asked.

"Whose story is this? Of course they had martinis then. They've always had martinis. Anyway, Dickens couldn't figure it out about this character in the book he was working on, so he asked for a martini. And the bartender yelled back, 'Olive or twist?' And that was how Dickens got the idea for *Oliver Twist*. Bartenders are real important."

"Somehow I don't believe that story," Richie said.

"Imagine what would have heppened if the bartender had asked Dickens, 'Peel or Onions?' You think there'd ever be a character named Peeler Onions? You think anybody'd do a

Broadway show named *Peeler*? Don't tell me. I know how important you are."

"You're a fountain of information," Richie said.

"That's because I have an inquiring mind," Trace said. "Fill this again, will you? Like, other people take things at face value, but I'm always searching, searching, searching."

"And now you're searching for ten thousand dollars."

"Fourteen," Trace said. "And don't remind me."

Just before eight P.M., the bartender handed him the telephone.

"Your room was empty," Elvira's voice said.

"Obviously."

"But I figured I'd find you there. Are you still going to take me out?"

"You've got it."

"I've got something good for you," she said.

"That's sort of what I was hoping," Trace said.

"Not like that. You're an animal. God, I love it." She paused and said, "I found out something about Paddington."

"Good. Where do we meet?"

"Too many people know me in town. I'll pick you up outside the motel in fifteen minutes. Look for a gray Mercedes."

"Naturally," Trace said. "Should I bring my own car?"

"Whatever for?"

"In case you make me walk home," Trace said.

"I won't," Elvira promised.

Elvira Patrick drank but couldn't drink. She had had two margaritas, hold the salt, and her voice was already slurred and thickening. On the other hand, Trace realized, he didn't know how many pitchers of Kool-Aid vodka mix she had consumed during the day.

They were in a small unfashionable cocktail lounge, just off the Merritt Parkway in Trumbull, Connecticut, about fifteen miles from Westport. There was an unfashionably good piano player working, singing unfashionable old songs about love and tenderness and caring which Elvira seemed to think translated into groping with her hands in Trace's lap.

"Easy there. Save some for later," Trace said.

Elvira giggled. Trace liked women who giggled, no matter what their age. It always seemed like an act of honesty. When Trace had been in the accounting business, he had worked with a businessman who reached down into his belly to laugh HO-HO-HO at almost everything, and it took Trace a while to realize that the phony laughter was meant to cover up the fact that the man didn't understand anything that was happening. He had been a personal manager for a lot of professionals, but he left stock certificates in subways and touted his clients into buying stocks in mining companies named after television cowboys. Not one of his clients had ever shown an annual profit in his portfolio, and whenever one complained, they got HO-HO-HO. To add to being dumb, he stole. That's when he laughed the hardest.

It had made Trace appreciate spontaneous gigglers. Nobody who giggled ever stole. That was one of Trace's laws of life.

Elvira folded her hands primly on the tabletop.

"So what did you find out today, Mr. Investigator?" she asked.

"Nothing."

"What a shame."

"It's pretty ordinary," Trace said. "Just your basic, run-of-the-mill, don't-find-out-a-damn-thing kind of day."

"A total waste of a day," she offered.

"Not total. I met you," Trace said.

"That's nice."

"I meant it to be," he said.

"Then I'll tell you what I found out," Elvira said.

"Make my day," Trace said.

Elvira took a deep breath, as if composing her rattled mind. It threatened to spill her bosom out of the top of her low-cut cocktail dress. She gripped the stem of her glass between the fingertips of both hands.

"All right," she said in a tone meant to be

businesslike. "I went into town today after you left and I got my face done."

"God did your face. If you paid anybody to meddle with it, you wasted your money," Trace said.

"Nice. Don't interrupt. You know my husband never compliments me?"

"Send him for an eye exam," Trace said.

"It's not that, it's just his work. Did you know he's a marriage counselor?"

"No."

"That's what he is. He deals all day with impotent men and sappy women and they drain his emotions. When he comes home on weekends, he doesn't have time for me. In case you're wondering why I fool around."

"I wasn't wondering," Trace said.

"Well, that's why. That, plus I have hot pants. I always did." She giggled again. "Anyway, after I was done with my face, I drove over to Wilton to see a friend of mine. Marylou. She's a writer."

"An ink-stained wretch," Trace said.

"A writer and a computer nerd," Elvira said.

"With pimples," Trace said. "All computer nerds have pimples."

"Marylou doesn't have pimples, except on her chest. That's the only part of her that's small. The rest of her is enormous. She's plain. Let's call her plain."

"And fat," Trace said. "Let's call her fat."

"Plain and fat," Elvira agreed. "That sounds like Marylou. We went to Wellesley together. She was always plain and fat. But she never had pimples and she was always real smart."

"Why'd you go see her?"

"Did I say she was a writer?" Elvira asked.

"You did."

"She writes stuff for the supermarket."

"You mean signs?" Trace asked. "Lowest prices anywhere? Buy nine and save?"

"No, not that. She writes for those newspapers they have in the supermarket. You know, Johnny and Liz, Together at Last. John Wayne's Ghost Rides the Hollywood Hills."

"Di's Tragic Battle with Herpes," Trace said.

"You've got it. She does that kind of stuff. Anyway, I figured that you people had probably done a lot of research."

"That's true," Trace said, thinking of the mountain of clippings Walter Marks had sent him.

"But I figured maybe you hadn't researched everything. I mean, most libraries don't carry copies of the *Supermarket Tattletale* or whatever the hell they're called."

"That's pretty clever. You're as smart as you are beautiful," Trace said.

"Thank you," Elvira said, flattered in the way that only a beautiful woman complimented on her brains can be flattered.

"So what did Marylou say?" Trace asked.

"I said that she's into computers?"

"Yes. My two loves, computers and super-market newspapers. God, what a fascinating woman she must be," Trace said.

"What she does is she puts everything that's in those stupid newspapers into computers," Elvira said.

"That's a particularly repulsive hobby," Trace said.

"It's not a hobby. It's her business. You know, how many stories can you make up, and you don't want to do a Johnny and Liz story when somebody else just did a Johnny and Liz story. You might want to do a Johnny and Charo story instead, if nobody did that. Or Liz and Dick, Closer in Death than They Were in Life. That's good and everybody does those, but you don't want to do them too fast, 'cause you want people to forget the last Liz and Dick story. You notice how in all those stories the headlines have question marks?"

"Right," Trace said.

"That's so that they can't get sued. Anyway, that's what Marylou says. If you say Richard Nixon's got herpes, he can sue you. But if you say Has Richard Nixon Got Herpes? he can't."

"Or else you can write Richard Nixon's Tragic Battle Against Herpes," Trace said.

"That's good too. That's the way it works," Elvira said. "So, anyway, I told Marylou that I wanted to know if there was anything in her

109

computers about Mrs. Paddington, and she just typed it on her computer, but first she did something with a telephone—like the computer was talking on the telephone, you know, with the phone lying next to the keyboard—and then just a few seconds later, there was writing on the little television screen they have on the computer."

"What'd the writing say?"

"It was two different stories. Marylou printed them for me." She fished in a silver clutch bag and brought out a piece of paper with ragged, computer-perforated edges. Trace reached for the paper, but Elvira pulled it closer to her and moved the candle on the table so she could see.

"They're both from eight years ago. The one says, 'In case anybody's wondering, that handsome man who's turning up at all the fancy restaurants with a string of starlets is none other than Helmsley Paddington, who made his bundle in pet products. Word is he may be planning to sink some of that bundle into a film project. Or maybe he just likes pets?' There's that question mark again. And here's the other one. 'Diners close by to the dark corner table at the posh Lazarus restaurant the other night had it all wrong when they thought they heard groans of ecstasy coming from the table. The way it was explained to us was that Helmsley Paddington, the pet-food jillionaire, and Shirlaine MacFonda, Hollywood sexpot, were just comparing animal calls. They met while both were working to save the whales. It wasn't heavy breathing, just whale impersonations. Thar she blows.' "

Elvira looked at Trace proudly and handed him the paper.

"How's that?" she asked.

"That's good stuff. Our detectives didn't find anything like that at all."

"Not too many people think to look in the supermarket news," Elvira said.

"I just wish I knew what to do with it," Trace said.

"You don't know?"

"No."

"Boy, are you dumb," she said. She finished her drink and waved to the waitress for another round at the table.

"Don't you see," she said. "Paddington didn't die in any accident. His wife murdered him because he was playing around. You don't have to pay up if she killed him, do you?"

"No. But you don't have any easier solution, do you?"

"What do you mean?" Elvira asked.

"It's tough solving a seven-year-old murder. You have anything that'll save my company money without me having to work so hard?"

Elvira snapped, "Well, that's the last time I ever do anything for you."

"Hold on," Trace said. "Just joking. This is

real good stuff. It gives me a whole new line of attack. I'm proud of you."

"Do I get a private detective's badge as your helper?"

"Would you settle for a decoder ring?" Trace asked. "Really, this is good stuff."

"Okay. Then that might not be the last time I ever do anything for you."

"I hope not," Trace said as he pocketed the paper with the stories on it.

Elvira was as beautiful with her clothes off as with them on, but back in bed with her at his motel room, Trace couldn't help feeling sorry for the woman.

She kept telling Trace "I love you," tossed casually into the conversation to avoid rebuff, and then waited for him to say the same thing back to her.

Trace wondered why some women, often beautiful women who seemed to have everything going for them, had such a low sense of esteem and self-worth that they needed random men telling them that they were loved. Were they starved of affection as children by their parents? Or was it unfeeling husbands?

It would have been very easy to say "I love you" back to Elvira, Trace thought. That was all she hungered for. It would have been easy to say and totally dishonest.

So he said it.

"I love you too," he said. What the hell. He owed her something. And maybe he would need her again. She was probably rich; maybe she had ten thousand dollars lying around in play money. Anyway, she could keep her eyes open and see if she could learn something about the Paddingtons. To hell with honesty; self-interest came first.

Elvira wasn't ready to let it go at that, unfortunately.

"No, you don't," she said.

"Okay," Trace said.

"No, really."

"Whatever you say," he said.

She tried another tack. "You're really good. I love making love to you."

"And I love making love to you," Trace said, repressing a sigh.

She held him tightly and did nice things with her body and oohed and aahed a lot, then tried again. "I love you," she whispered in his ear in a paroxysm of frenzy.

"I love you too," he said again.

This time she didn't question it.

After she left, Trace got out the bottle of vodka he had bought at the cocktail lounge in Trumbull and sat at the small table in the motel room. He turned on the television set but left the sound off.

Then he got up and put on his underwear.

He always wondered why he insisted upon wearing his underwear even though he was alone and not likely to be unalone.

He could never figure it out. Maybe it was some fear of a flash fire. If the building caught fire, he would at least be able to run out without first looking for clothes to put on. It was bad enough being a pauper, but being a pauper, standing in front of a burning motel, with kindly policemen wrapping a blanket around his naked cold body was more than he could take.

Wearily, his mouth thick with too many cigarettes, his head thick with too much vodka, he started to dictate into the golden-frog microphone on his tape recorder.

9

Trace's Log: Devlin Tracy in the matter of Helmsley Paddington, Four A.M. Tuesday, Tape Number One.

Hello, tape recorder, old friend. My only friend.

This is what you've driven me to, Chico. I'm sitting here, oversmoked, overdrunk, my natural juices all gone from my body because you wouldn't lend me the ten thousand dollars I needed when I needed it. Well, fourteen thousand.

I like to think that if you had but known what it would do to me, you might have acted differently. That you might have said, "Trace, sure, I'll lend you the fourteen thousand. More than that if you need it. I'll buy half your interest in the restaurant." I really like to think that,

Chico, because I'd really like to give you one more chance to show that you're a worthwhile person.

But I won't call you anymore. I'm finished with that. You can call and tell me if you want.

In the meantime, you've got me reduced to this. Drinking, smoking, rutting with a total stranger. God, I hope you hear this tape. I'm going to put it in a metal box so that if this place goes afire and I incinerate because I was busy looking for my underwear, the tape will still be there for your ears to hear. I'll leave a message on it that it goes right to you, forget Walter Marks.

That's right, Chico. In the sack with a strange woman, all to try to make some money from this stupid Paddington case. God, I hate this kind of work.

Tonight wasn't all a waste, though. While I was making love to Elvira—do you hear me, Chico? Long slow sensuous love—I had this wonderful idea.

I bet I could make a lot of money if I printed up a little button that said, "I'll tell you I love you." No, the hell with a button. A gold-plated lapel pin. Might as well go the whole route.

You probably wouldn't realize it because you're so filled with yourself that you don't think you need anybody, but this button would make men who wear it the scourge of singles bars or networking centers or wherever it is that men go now to pick up women.

Because I have found out a great truth. Most of the women who jump into the sack at the twitch of an eyebrow do it only so that someone will say to them, "I love you."

So you get a lapel pin to identify the men who'll do that and it would make a lot of men and women happy. Men because they wouldn't have to waste money on false alarms, women because they'd know in advance they were getting what they wanted.

This is a wonderful idea, Chico, and when it is successful and I am rolling in wealth, don't ask me for any money. If your sister's plumbing breaks down again or your Japanese mother decides to take English lessons—and it's about time too—don't look to me for the money. I'm going to keep it all, every damned last cent of it, and invest it in restaurants. I know, the failure rate for new restaurants is seventy-five percent, but I'm going to change all that.

Revenge. Ahhhh, revenge. Who said that it was a dish best eaten cold? Just when you think I've forgiven and forgotten, I'm going to stomp down on your ass. You'll see. You'll get yours. My day will come. *Der tag.* You'll see.

But in the meantime, I am reduced to this. Reduced to worrying about lovable Helmsley Paddington and his buck-toothed wife, Nadine, who have devoted their lives to getting rich off animals. That's right, world. Rich. I don't buy that love-the-animals bullshit. I think people love animals because they want to get something out of it. If you own a dog, you can't afford a wife but you want affection anyway from some dumb brute. You own birds because they prettify the house, fish because watching them is cheaper than watching television. You own a cat because something deep inside you craves the smell of urine on ashes.

So I think that Hemmie and Nadine, yeah, maybe they liked animals some, but basically they were in business. Quick. How many dogs does Nadine Paddington have now? Answer. Zero. With that big place in Westport and two servants, answer, zero.

So much for love, puppy or otherwise. And when Helmsley Paddington flew off, seven years ago, on a flight to save the seals, I wouldn't bet that he didn't have a deal to sell artificial seal coats and he was just trying to dry up the competition. And then no more of him. That's all.

And now Nadine wants her two million dollars in insurance.

Let's see how that scans.

Big house in Westport, standard. Two cars in the garage, one a gray Mercedes, standard. Two servants, standard.

Well, maybe not standard. Anything involving Ferd is definitely substandard. Ferd is the guard or caretaker or whatever he is, and he looks like Sergeant Slaughter, the wrestler. Somehow he took a dislike to me right away and for the life of me, I can't understand why. Maybe he doesn't like the way I sing "Abdul the Bulbul Emir." Holy Mother, is it time for new material? But anyway, my charm got me in to see Nadine.

Nadine, I guess, is pretty sick. I saw a wheelchair under the stairs. She's got pinkeye. I thought only babies got pinkeye. And I guess she's distraught. If I had teeth like that woman and my spouse died, I'd be distraught too. But I'd still go and get my teeth fixed.

Hemmie, she said, was an exceptional man and they were as happy as clams. And then he vanished and she waited seven years for him to come home. Maybe she's a Greta Garbo fan. She wants to be alone. Anyway, that's why she moved out of New Hampshire, this all happened then, and went to Westport, where she lives with Ferd, ugly and nasty, no dogs, and Maggie, maid, unseen, but if she's beautiful I'm going to pork her, Chico, because what else do I have in my life?

Anyway, I couldn't find out anything from Nadine, except that she spent too much time in the sun when she was younger 'cause the skin on her face is all cracked like an old wallet.

I've got an awful lot of work to do to try to prove something in this case. I guess it'd be

easier if there was something to prove. Nadine
Paddington isn't the insurance-scam type. Her
husband, I don't know. A good-looking man
can twist a homely woman around his finger—I
know that firsthand, Chico—but I don't know.

Nadine's a hermit anyway. They turned down
the next-door neighbor's garbanzo loaf, although
that might not mean anything more than ram-
pant good taste still lives.

That was neighbor one. She jogged up and
down while we were talking. Neighbor two,
Chico, that was Elvira, the one I slept with
tonight. She and I hit it right off. She tantalized
me in a bikini, and even without knowing me
real well, I know she would have lent me the
ten thousand or fourteen thousand dollars I
need, but she was a little short of spending
money this month.

A nice woman too. Her husband's a marriage
counselor and works in New York and has a
mistress there. Elvira and the girlfriend have
lunch together. Isn't that cozy? I wonder what
Bart, the husband, thinks about having two
women comparing him over a lunch table. Jeez.

She invited me to take her out and then she
told me good stuff. How Helmsley Paddington
was doing the Hollywood wealthy-investor number and romancing starlets. Elvira says that's an
angle.

It goes like this. Hemmie is out sporting on
Bucky Beaver, the wife. He's not terribly dis-

creet about it because his name winds up in supermarket newspapers. And Nadine finds out and gets so damned mad that when he goes to save the seals, she sticks a bomb on his plane and sends him to that big igloo in the sky.

Motive. An ugly woman scorned always has a motive.

Aaaaah, why am I jerking myself off? I don't believe Nadine Paddington's a killer. And even if she was, how am I going to prove anything about a murder seven years ago? I have trouble finding the ashtray in a rental car, now I'm going to find a seven-year-old clue? Forget it.

Maybe I will just con Mrs. Paddington into coming out and liquor her up and make love to her. I'll wear my lapel pin that says 'I'll tell you I love you' and she'll fall at my feet. I'll kiss her from the side to avoid collision and I'll wangle the truth out of her.

If I can get her out. She doesn't go out much. That's what everybody says, including Adam Shapp—he's her lawyer. She types him neat little notes. Probably on paper with puppies' pictures on it.

So that's the case, and if that wasn't enough to make it a terrible day, that bandit, Eddie, wants fourteen thousand to fix the restaurant. And he's trying to sell out himself. What a pain in the balls that is. Never do business in New Jersey. I should have learned that a long time ago.

I think I'm getting ripped off and every penny I have in the world, forty thousand, is in that place. I hate the restaurant business. Seventy-five percent of all new restaurants fail.

I'm going to apply for one of those grants that they give every year to big thinkers to give them a chance to do their work without having to worry about making a living.

The Japanese declare people national treasures and venerate them. For your information, Chico, even though you're partly one of them, the Japanese won't declare you a national treasure. Maybe the national treasury, you cheap thing, but not a treasure.

But why doesn't America do that? Why doesn't someone come up and give me money and say we know you've got a large and really important mind and we want you to brainstorm for the next five years without having to worry about making a living. The things I could invent with such freedom. The questions I could answer. I could find out how airport restaurants can turn bread into brown toast without ever getting it warm. I have this idea for a great new product. A combination mouthwash and after-shave; one big bottle to do both things. Travelers would go crazy for it.

More big questions. Why can't you find a mailbox on the street outside the main New York City post office? Important questions, and I could answer them if I had the time.

Never mind. I'm plugging through on this case, Chico. My day will come and you are not going to share in it. Trust me.

Anyway, I think tomorrow I'm going to do some checking up on good old Hemmie Paddington and find out if there were any skeletons in the closet that might make his wife want to murder him. How I'll prove that, though, I'll never know.

And I won't have much time tomorrow. It's five A.M. now, maybe even later, and I've just finished making love to a beautiful redheaded woman and it was wonderful, Chico, wonderful. She told me she loved me. And I believe her.

Most people do, you know. Except for those who are cheap and tightfisted and think that anyone who's nice to them is trying to borrow money.

I drank and smoked too much today. That's the good news. Somehow I forgot to eat. I'll think about that tomorrow.

It's all your fault, Chico. If I do die in a fire, with or without underwear, and you get this tape, make sure the insurance company reimburses my estate for my expenses.

I did almost everything today by credit card, except tonight I spent a hundred and fifty dollars on cocktails with Elvira. You hear that, Chico? A hundred and a half. I spend money like water on people who deserve it.

And I guess I spent another fifty dollars on

miscellaneous things. So make it two hundred dollars. Hell, round it off. Two-fifty. Deduct a dollar for the cheap ballpoint pens I stole today from the lawyer's office. Two-forty-nine.

Chico, make sure my estate collects. But don't go looking for any of it yourself, because I'm writing you out of my will. That'll fix you.

Devlin Tracy signing off.

10

"Hi, Sarge. How goes it?"

"What's wrong, son?"

"What do you mean what's wrong? Does something have to be wrong for me to call my only father? How's the private detecting business?"

"Not bad. I got a big industrial client who wants me to find out who's stealing paper clips and I'm starting to get a few regular cases."

"What's a regular case?"

"You know, missing husbands, cheating wives, that kind of things. It's starting to go real well."

"Let's get down to the important stuff," Trace said. "Is it getting you out of the house?"

"Yes. Every blessed day," Sarge said.

"Praise be God."

"So what's wrong?" Trace's father asked again.

"I really resent it when people think there's got to be something wrong when I call them," Trace said.

"When you start resenting things, I *know* something's wrong. Besides, you sound like death warmed over."

"I've been drinking too much," Trace said.

"Why?" Sarge asked.

"I need ten thousand dollars," Trace said.

"A sex-change operation? At your age?"

"Not until I get this one down right first," Trace said. "You got ten thousand dollars?"

"No," Sarge said. "Every penny I had is in the new agency. You know how much office chairs cost?"

"For Christ's sakes, Sarge. You didn't have to go wasting your money on chairs and stuff. Didn't you ever learn the joy of being frugal?"

"The last time you were here, you told me my office looked like a locker room," Sarge said.

"I said it smelled like a locker room. A seventy-nine-cent can of air freshener would have done just as good as new chairs. And anyway, you don't have to take everything to heart. If you spend all your money everytime somebody complains, what are you going to have left for a rainy day?"

"Hopes for sunny and clearing," Sarge said. "Listen, I don't have the ten, but I can get it."

"From the sharks?" Trace asked.

"Of course, from the sharks. Where else would I get ten thousand dollars?"

"Pop, if I wanted to go to the loan sharks, I'd go myself," Trace said. "I don't need you to go for me."

"Then why don't you go and get the ten thousand from the sharks?"

" 'Cause I can't pay it back," Trace said.

"Well, I've got to admit it," Sarge said. "That's a new wrinkle in borrowing. It might make it a little tough for you at first, until people catch on to your new system."

"You're not being helpful," Trace said. "I'll be able to pay it back eventually. Just not right away. And not on any schedule."

"Look," Sarge said. "I could get it from the sharks and I could pay it back. Then when you get it, you can pay me back."

"Naaah, I don't like dealing with middlemen. You think Mother's got ten thousand?"

"Probably, but she wouldn't lend it to you," Sarge said.

"Why not? I'm her son."

"She doesn't trust you," Sarge said.

"I said I'm her son, I didn't say I was trustworthy. What has trust got to do with anything?"

"Got me," Sarge said. "She wouldn't lend me anything to start this business, I don't think she'll lend you money for a sex-change operation."

"I'd bet she'd lend it to one of those idiotic cousins I've got," Trace said.

"What cousin?"

"I don't know. Try Bruce. They're all named Bruce."

"I imagine she'd lend it to Bruce," Sarge said.

"Why would she lend it to a nephew and not to me?" Trace demanded.

"It hasn't got anything to do with you, except that she doesn't really like you. Ever since you got divorced."

"That's why she doesn't like me?"

"Don't feel bad. She doesn't like anybody. She doesn't like Cousin Bruce either."

"But she'd lend him the money," Trace said.

"Not because of him. It'd just be to show her relatives that she can afford to lend somebody ten thousand dollars. Your mother is a very prideful woman."

"If she lends it to me, I'll promise her that I'll tell all the relatives. I'll send them telegrams and Mass cards."

"Hold the Mass cards," Sarge said. "All the relatives are Jewish."

"All right, scrap the Mass cards. You think it'll work?"

"No. She still won't lend it to you."

"I shouldn't even ask?" Trace said. "What can she do except refuse?"

"You underestimate your mother. First of all, she'll refuse for sure. But then, she'll always remember. For the rest of your life, you're going to hear her telling everybody about the time you tried to get her to give you her last ten thousand dollars, which would have put her in poverty and taken away all her security because, well, you know, her husband drinks and no one seems to care about whether she lives or dies in her old age, not like some children who seem to care about their—"

"Enough, enough," Trace said. "You're bringing tears to my eyes."

"Did you try borrowing from Chico?" Sarge asked.

"Of course I did. She was my first hope. She wouldn't lend it to me."

"Why not?" Sarge asked.

"She said I'd lose it."

"Got a good head on her shoulders, that girl," Sarge said. "If you married her, maybe under the law you'd have a right to loot her savings account."

"I'll have to think about that," Trace said. "It's not a bad idea. Anyway, I just called to see how things were. I'm glad you're all right."

"Mother and I are both fine. I'm out working, so I'm happy, and she's staying home, complaining about being neglected, so she's happy. What do you need ten thousand dollars for?"

"I invested in a restaurant. Some start-up expenses that I didn't expect."

"A new restaurant?" Sarge asked.

"Yes," Trace said. "Down the Jersey shore."

"Did you know that seventy-five percent of all new restaurants go under?" Sarge asked.

"No fooling, Pop. I never heard that."

"It's true, son."

"I'll never forget it again. Give my love to Mother."

"You're not going to call her?"

"Of course not. I never call her," Trace said.

"Hey, if I win the Pick-Six lottery, I'll give you the ten grand outright," Sarge said.

"I'll hold you to that," Trace said. "Try fourteen grand."

Trace pressed the handset button with a finger, dropped the receiver on the bed alongside him, and lit a cigarette. This was getting serious. Chico wouldn't give it up, Sarge didn't have it, and the only one left was Bob Swenson, the president of Garrison Fidelity, and that was a dead end without making a telephone call. Despite being a millionaire, Swenson never had any money. He was always stiffing Trace on bar tabs and hotel bills. Any money he might have in his pocket, he always spent on women. He frequently complained to Trace that his money was tied up.

"When does it get untied?" Trace once asked him.

"The minute I die. Then watch my wife untangle the twisted web of my finances. She'll have me liquidated before I'm cold. Until then,

I can't touch anything. It's the only reason I don't leave that woman."

There was nobody else. There was no hope. It was all over.

When disappointed, lash out. That was Trace's philosophy. He called Walter Marks' office at Garrison Fidelity.

"Let me talk to Groucho," he told the woman who answered.

"I beg your pardon," the woman said.

"You're new there, aren't you?" Trace asked.

"Who is this calling?"

"You know how I know you're new? Because only the new ones ask 'who' when I ask for Groucho. Walter Marks. Groucho. I want to talk to him."

"And you are?"

"Trace. Devlin Tracy. And now you're going to say that you'll see if he's in. Trust me, he's in. Just punch this call right into his office."

"I'll see if he's in, sir," the young woman's voice said coldly.

The secretary put him on hold. Trace hung up.

He got up and finally unpacked his clothes. He put his kit of toilet articles in the bathroom and wondered why everybody laughed when he suggested that someone manufacture a joint mouthwash and after-shave lotion.

He found an ice-cube machine in the hall and put some ice cubes and the rest of his dwindling vodka supply into a plastic water glass.

He sang three choruses of "Finlandia, Finlandia All the Way," lit a cigarette, smoked it, and tossed it into the butt can, then lit another. He turned on a soap opera, but after three minutes, despairing of ever understanding any of it, he turned it off and dialed Marks' number again.

"Hello," said the same woman's voice. "Mr. Marks' office."

"Hello, my dear," said Trace, dripping oil. "My name is Devlin Tracy and I would enjoy greatly the honor of speaking with Mr. Walter Marks if you would be so kind as to put me through."

"Did you just call?"

"I?"

"It was you, it was you, and when he wanted to talk to you, you weren't on the line, you hung up, and he yelled at me for cutting you off."

"Do not worry, my dear. I will set things aright."

"Thank you," she said.

"But that's what you get for being a peckerhead," Trace said.

Marks' voice clicked onto the line. "Who you calling a peckerhead?" he demanded.

"Not you, Walter, old friend. It would be too hard to explain. Why don't we just let the subject drop?"

"All right. Let it drop. What did you want?"

"I just wanted to report in and tell you that everything is going swimmingly on the Paddington case," Trace said.

"Really? You figure out yet how you're going to save us two million dollars?"

"I expect a major breakthrough in a day or two," Trace said.

"Are you serious? Is there something there? He's alive, isn't he? That prick is alive and trying to steal money from us."

"Right now," Trace said unctuously, "I could speak naught but supposition to you. In a few days, I should have everything tied up."

"That'll be real good if you can do it," Marks said.

"Yes. The other side seems to be impressed also," Trace said.

"What do you mean?"

"Just that . . . Well, it was made clear to me by certain people involved in this matter that perhaps certain silences on my part might lead to financial reward later on."

"You mean they're trying to bribe you?" Marks demanded.

"I couldn't really comment on that at this time."

"How can they do that? The nerve of those bastards. How can they do that? The nerve of those bastards. How can they do that? Who did it?"

"Perhaps they inspected my bank balance," Trace said. "Perhaps they've heard that I am in a small financial pinch right now and could use some monetary assistance."

"Monetary assistance?" There was a long pause, then Marks said, "Wait a minute. Are you trying to con me into lending you money for that bound-to-fail restaurant?"

"Did I mention a restaurant to you?" Trace asked.

"No. That's why I'm suspicious."

"I don't need any money from you," Trace said. "In fact, in the near future I may never need money again. And as for the restaurant, I would rather not be involved in any project that has you associated with it, however slightly."

"Well, I'm glad of that," Marks said.

"On the other hand, I might be more resistant to temptation if I had an advance on my retainer," Trace said.

"Your retainer's already been paid six months in advance. As soon as I did that, you started talking about quitting. Not a chance."

"How about paying me in advance for this Paddington case?"

"You haven't found out anything yet and I want you to know that I don't believe for a minute your bullshit about being on the verge of a great discovery. We had detectives, real detectives, look into that case and they couldn't find anything. I just put you on it so you'll at least do something for your retainer."

"Real detectives, Groucho, huh?"

"That's right. Real detectives. With license and so forth."

"Your goddamn detectives couldn't find a freaking bass drum in a phone booth," Trace snapped.

"How's that?"

"They never found out, did they, these real detectives, that Helmsley Paddington was the big man around town in Hollywood? They never found out that he was out traipsing around with Hollywood starteenies while Mrs. P. was home minding the dogs. They didn't find that out, did they?"

"I never heard that," Marks said.

"Of course, you didn't. You know so little, Groucho. But I, Devlin Tracy, I know all."

"I'll believe it and you when I see something concrete."

"I'd like to see something concrete. Wrapped around your ankles," Trace said. "As you bubble downward."

"Sticks and stones may break my bones," Marks started.

"And concrete boots can kill you," Trace said.

"I don't want to listen to any more of this. I think you're drunk."

"Well, listen to this for a moment. That big

goddamn package you gave me with the file on the Paddingtons . . ."

"Yes."

"It didn't have their insurance application. I need their doctor's name in New Hampshire."

"All right. Hold on and I'll look for it."

"No," Trace said. "I've got other things to do. You get it and ship it up here by messenger. Leave it at the desk of Ye Olde English Motel. Groucho, I'll never forgive you for making me stay in a place like this. I'll pick it up when I get back from my travels today."

"Travels? Going somewhere?" Marks asked.

"Always on the job," Trace said.

"I'll have the stuff delivered. It should have been in the folder."

"It wasn't."

"Are you sure? Or did you just overlook it?"

"I would much rather have looked hard for it than to have to talk to you on the phone and ruin an otherwise perfect day," Trace said.

"You'll have it today," Marks said.

"Thank you, Groucho."

"And don't call me Groucho to my secretaries anymore."

Trace hung up.

He took a shower and, when he came out of the bathroom, saw that the level of vodka in his bottle was perilously low. He knew the motel didn't have room service, but he called the front desk to see if someone was available for running an errand. He dialed the three-digit number and let it ring ten times before hanging up. Then he dialed the hotel operator and got no answer from her either. Finally, he dialed nine, got a local line, and dialed the motel's outside telephone number.

The operator answered on the first ring.

"Ye Olde English Motel," she said.

"Is this motel in operation?" Trace asked.

"I beg your pardon?"

"This is Mr. Tracy in three-seventeen. Is there someone around who can run an errand for me? Go to the store?"

"I'm afraid not, sir."

"I'll pay somebody for it," Trace said.

"There isn't anybody available. But the shopping center is just across the street."

"You don't understand. I can't go out in the daylight," Trace said.

"I'm sorry," the woman sniffed. "The liquor store delivers, however. Their number is 555-0029."

"Thank you. You've been very helpful," Trace said.

How did she know I wanted the liquor store? he wondered as he dialed the number. He ordered two quarts of Finlandia delivered to his room.

As an afterthought, he asked, "Do you sell any food there?"

"Just junk," the clerk said. "Potato chips, like that."

"Peanuts?"

"We've got peanuts."

"Send over six bags of peanuts," Trace said. "Bags, not cans. And smoked sausages. You got Slim Jims?"

"Right."

"Send over two of those."

"Two, sir?"

"Yes. I'm trying to gain weight."

Trace was watching the six-o'clock news, trying to make sense of the incomprehensible jumble of Connecticut place-names, when the telephone rang. It was Elvira.

"Am I still your deputy sheriff?" she asked.

"Shore are, podner," Trace said.

"Okay. I thought you'd be interested in this. I just saw what's her name, Maggie, leaving the Paddington house in the red station wagon."

"Oh?"

"She's headed your way. That road exits right at your motel. I thought you might want to keep an eye on her."

"Thanks," Trace said.

"Give me a call later. Maybe we can get together."

"Okay," Trace said as he hung up.

Should he try to follow Maggie or not? He'd rather stay in the room and drink and watch television. The A-Team was going to be on tonight. He thought about it for a moment, but even while he was thinking, he was taping the small recorder to his waist and slipping into his shoes.

Four minutes later, he was sitting in his car, the engine running, just inside the entrance to the motel's parking lot. The red Saab station wagon drove by and Trace turned out into traffic following her.

She made a right turn onto the Post Road, drove only a half-mile, and turned into the driveway of a large bowling alley.

Bowling? Trace hoped not. The clatter of ball against pins was more than his head could take.

He sat in his parked car and watched Maggie get out of the Saab. She was tall, blond, and very beautiful. She was wearing a body suit and sneakers, and Trace thought it didn't look like any bowling apparel he had ever seen.

When she went to the door of the bowling alley, he left the car and followed her. Just inside the door, he saw a sign that said HETTIE'S HEALTH SPA with an arrow pointing upstairs. He glanced through the glass doors leading to the bowling alley, but did not see Maggie at the manager's counter, so he walked upstairs.

A pretty young clerk sat behind a desk just inside the door to the spa. The spa itself seemed to be one large room with several Universal machines, some heavy weights, and treadmills and specialized body-building equipment along the walls. A half-dozen people, both men and women, were working out, but he saw no Maggie.

The clerk smiled at him inquisitively.

"Just came up to look around," Trace said. "Do you have a brochure or something on your prices?"

It took him a moment or two to explain to the clerk that he was not interested in lifetime, annual, semiannual, quarterly, monthly, or per-visit membership, but just wanted to look at a brochure. When she finally surrendered one, he sat down in a chair that commanded a view of the spa and pretended to look at it.

"Exactly which of our facilities are you interested in?" she asked. "Mister . . .?"

"Marks. Walter Marks," Trace said. "Basically, I'm interested in redeveloping my trapezius muscles. I used to have the best trapeziuses when I was in college, but I've slipped."

"Trapeziuses go real quickly," the clerk agreed. "Our Universal machines are wonderful for that."

"Well, I'll probably need something," Trace said. "I built them up in my family's circus act. Maybe you heard of us? The Flying Markses?"

"No. I'm afraid not."

"That's all right. We're not as famous as we used to be when we were with Ringling Brothers. I was good then, but I got too big for the act. My father couldn't catch me anymore."

"Oh, I'm sorry."

Trace saw Maggie come into the exercise area from a plain door. It must have been a women's locker room, Trace decided, because she was now barefoot. She was wearing brown-tinted designer glasses and she looked very beautiful. She went instantly to a miniature trampoline and began jumping up and down. She looked nice bobbing up and down. Certainly a lot better than her next-door neighbor.

"I'd like to look around at the equipment," Trace said. "Is that all right?"

"Sure, Mr. Marks. You're familiar with this equipment?"

"Absolutely."

"Okay. If you have any questions, just ask me. I'm Connie."

Feeling very out of place in his jacket and tie, Trace sauntered slowly around the gym, occasionally pretending to test a piece of equipment, slowly working his way toward Maggie.

She was doing military presses on a weight machine when he sauntered up and clicked on his tape recorder. He stopped in front of her and said, "You come here often?" He gave her his most winning smile.

He got nothing in return. No smile, no comment. Just more presses. Was every woman in Westport either a nymphomaniac or an exercise freak? he wondered.

He perched on the seat of the machine next

to hers and made a halfhearted effort to press the bar, which was at his shoulder height. He couldn't even move it.

"I'm thinking of joining the spa," he said.

He waited.

"How's membership here? Do you like it?"

He waited.

"Would you recommend the lifetime membership or the monthly?"

He waited.

"I'm sorry about your affliction," he said. "But many people have been known to get their voices back overnight."

She snapped her head toward him. He could only see her eyes slightly through the tinted glasses, but he knew they were glaring at him.

"Leave me alone," she spat out in a voice that was not much louder than a whisper.

"Well, that's a start," Trace said. "Keep it up. Soon you'll be inviting me for drinks. Chatting away into the wee hours. Making small talk like the grown-ups."

Without another word, Maggie Winters got up from the machine and walked briskly away. She pushed her way through the door into the women's locker room. It closed silently behind her.

Trace went back to the anteroom and to kill some time filled out an application for a lifetime membership at a fee of only three thousand dollars in the name of Walter Marks. He gave

Marks' home address and asked that the bill be sent there.

Connie, the clerk, looked at the application and said, "You live in New York?"

"Yes. But I spend most of the summer and my weekends in Westport."

"We could bill you at your Westport address," she said.

"No. That varies. Tax reasons, it's better to get the bill in New York." He winked. "You know, get my favorite big uncle to pay for half the membership."

"Okay, Mr. Marks. Whatever you want."

There was no sign of Maggie, so Trace went downstairs to wait. He sat in his car watching the front entrance to the bowling-alley building, and when he saw her come out, he walked quickly toward the red Saab.

"Miss Winters," he called out.

She looked up from the car door as he approached, then made a hurried effort to unlock the car.

"I just wanted to talk to you for a few moments," Trace said.

He felt a heavy hand on his shoulder.

As he spun around, a fist crashed into his jaw. He saw sparkles of stars behind his eyes. He winced from the pain. He was hit again on the other side of the face. He felt consciousness passing as he dropped toward the pavement. For good measure he felt a shoe kick him in the left side. Hard. He groaned once and brought his hands up to his side. A voice exhaled, "Leave us alone," then Trace heard a car door slam, a motor start nearby, and then tires rolling over stones.

He opened his eyes and got up to a sitting position. His ribs felt as if they were on fire. The red Saab was leaving the parking lot.

Trace got to his feet and carefully touched his ribs. They were sore, but nothing seemed broken. He took a deep breath without added pain. No lungs punctured. He looked out at the road, but the red Saab was long gone.

Trace walked slowly back to his own car. Somehow, he was getting the impression that Maggie Winters didn't want to talk to him.

Back in his room, Trace undressed, took a shower, and then surveyed the damage. He had a mouse growing under his left eye and a bruise on the right side of his jaw. His lower ribs on the left side were tender and swollen, but nothing was broken.

He put on his underwear, sneaked out into the hallway to get ice from the ice chest, came back inside, and settled down with a drink.

He watched the end of the *Tuesday Night Movie* and the late news. He turned on Johnny Carson, hoping for Joan Rivers, but instead he got Johnny Carson, so he turned on *Nightline* and watched Ted Koppel skewer a diplomat from India.

He decided a recovering body needed nourishment, so he ate a bag of peanuts and a Slim Jim. It hurt him to chew.

He finished one bottle of Finlandia and started on the next. He watched Vincent Price and Peter Lorre trying to frighten each other in a movie that would have frightened no one except Edgar Allan Poe, who was blamed for the story.

Finally, he took his tape recorder and microphone from the top of the dresser.

11

Trace's Log: Devlin Tracy in the matter of the
Paddingtons, two A.M. Wednesday, Tape Number Two. One tape in the master file.

Nothing much to report today because I only
left my room once and then just for a few minutes to get the shit kicked out of me. The tape
has me trying to be charming with Maggie Winters and her telling me to leave her alone. It
probably has me grunting as I got hit and kicked,
but I don't know. I didn't have the heart to play
it back.

I am swimming in crap soup. My forty thousand dollars is buried in that submersible New
Jersey restaurant and is going to float away and
no one will give me the money I need to keep
alive.

One vodka bottle is empty and the other one's

threatening. I don't think I drank that much. I think Finlandia evaporates faster than other vodka. I have to check this out. Maybe I can invent an evaporation meter or something. For the wary consumer.

I don't think anybody's going to give me ten thousand dollars for it, though. I have to get to work tomorrow. This being an entrepreneur is tough.

I guess it was Ferd who kicked the shit out of me, but I don't know why. I don't want to think about it. Tomorrow is another day. Maggie Winters is pretty, Chico, real pretty, and I'm sure when I have more time to work on her, I'll have her eating out of my hand.

Oooops, spilled my drink. Damn, it's on the rug, unsalvageable. I'll blot it up later. I have so many things on my mind. So many things. Goooooddd . . .

12

There might be more boring places in the world than New Hampshire. Trace was willing to give the state the benefit of every doubt, but only because he had not been to every other place in the world. The state, as he drove through it and through it, was kind of like Tulsa, Oklahoma, only bumpier and bigger. But it was possible that Switzerland was worse. Trace had never been to Switzerland. Holland must be a beaut. Iceland too. North Dakota had to be high up on any list, and Tibet must be a drag.

But New Hampshire was in their league.

Trace ached for the whole four-hour drive, along the Connecticut and Massachusetts turnpikes. He always traveled with surgical tape, which he used to tape his recording machine under his clothing, so he had used it to tape his ribs tightly.

A Band-Aid under his left eye hid 60 percent of the bruise there. His jaw was still sore. But he was alive, and if he hadn't been going through New Hampshire, he might have felt like celebrating.

The town of West Hampstead was more of the same. The name of the Paddington's doctor in West Hampstead was Alphonse Bigot, and Trace wondered who the hell had a name like Bigot.

He found the doctor's house-cum-office on the far edge of the town. It was a California-style house, all natural weathered wood and glass and porches and decks. Trace had a theory that people like to see that their doctors are successful and rich, sort of on the theory that seventy million sick Frenchmen can't be wrong. In that case, he thought, Bigot's patients must be delighted.

Trace parked and walked up the chipped-stone path to the large house. A door next to the garage was marked office, but when he got closer he saw a sign that read: HOURS MONDAY, TUESDAY, THURSDAY, FRIDAY, SATURDAY. BY APPOINTMENT ONLY.

Damn. It was Wednesday. Doctor's day off. Now, where would he find an Alphonse Bigot, M.D., in West Hampstead, New Hampshire, on a Wednesday? Golf course? Tennis courts?

Boating? Sitting around the stove at the corner grocery?

He rang the door bell, but there was no answer. He tried to peer in the two-car garage, but the windows were painted over.

He was about to leave when he heard a sound that seemed to come from the back of the house. There was an eight-foot-high gate in a tall wooden fence whose color matched that of the house and its shingles. Trace tried the gate. It pushed open easily and he found himself on a broad wooden deck that was pretty but totally unnecessary because it was elevated only six inches above the ground level, and the same white stone used in the driveway could just as easily have been used for a walkway around the house.

As he walked toward the back, he could see that the house stood alone atop the small hill, surrounded first by the tall high fence and then by a cluster of thick pines.

The sound he had heard was laughter.

Two people laughing. They sat in a wooden hot tub drinking from crystal champagne glasses. Trace assumed they were naked, although the water bubbling in the tub made it impossible to see clearly. From the woman's cleavage, though, he guessed she was naked or was wearing nothing but pasties. She was blond, with that platinum color found naturally only in albino mutations. Her hair was piled up loosely atop her head and stray tendrils curled along the sides of her pretty but over-made-up face. Her skin was delicately tanned, and she wore heavy red nailpolish.

The man sitting alongside her looked as if he had been weaned on carpeting. Heavy black hair covered his chest, his back, and his shoulders, and as was so often the case, his head was at least semibald because he was wearing a hairpiece that Howard Cosell might have rejected.

He finished clinking his glass with the woman's and sipped. His other hand was under the water. Soft music played from a portable tape deck a few feet from the wooden-walled tub.

The man looked up suddenly and saw Trace.

"Hey. Who are you? What the hell do you want here?"

"I'm looking for Dr. Bigot. Sorry to intrude."

"Off today. Can't you see the sign out front? Get out of here."

The woman slid down in the water so her breasts were totally submerged. Trace had the feeling that if waited long enough she might pop to the top like a navy mine.

"Are you Dr. Bigot?"

"It's Big-O. Big-O. It's French. Will you get out of here?"

Trace decided the man was naked, or else he would have jumped up and taken a run at Trace. It was hard to make a threatening run when you were in the altogether.

"My name's Tracy. I'm from the Garrison Fidelity Insurance Company."

"I've got all the insurance I need. G'wan, get out of here."

"Garrison Fidelity. I think my office told you I was coming."

"Oh, yeah. Garrison Fidelity. You're Tracy?"

"That's right."

"I talked to a Mr. Marks. He said you'd be a troublesome pain in the ass."

"I find that hard to believe," Trace said.

"I don't. So what do you want?"

"You're Dr. Bigot, right?"

"Right."

"I wanted to talk to you about the Paddingtons."

"Helmsley and Nadine?"

"You know any other Paddingtons?" Trace asked.

"All right, I guess I've got to talk to you. What the hell happened to your face?"

"I got beat up," Trace said.

"Jumping into somebody else's backyard?" Bigot asked.

"I never got as far as the backyard," Trace said.

"All right. This is Nurse Teddy, my nurse." He clapped a big hairy hand on the blonde's slim shoulder. Trace nodded at her and she smiled back.

"Look, it's hard to talk to you hovering out

there," Bigot said. "Why don't you take off your clothes and sit in here with us?"

"Yes, why not?" Nurse Teddy said.

Trace, remembering the tape recorder whirring on his hip, said, "No, I can't."

"Why not?"

"I've got herpes," Trace said. "This doctor I know in La Jolla said that hot tub temperature can keep the virus alive indefinitely. I'd better not."

"You're damn right, you'd better not," Bigot said. "Thanks for telling me."

"My pleasure."

"So I guess you're wondering what we're doing here?" Bigot said.

"I came to talk to you, remember?" Trace said.

"I mean Teddy and me."

"That's your business," Trace said.

"That's a good attitude. People around here are very bigoted and narrow-minded."

"Anti-Bigot?" Trace said.

"Big-O. French," Bigot said.

"Okay. Let's talk about Paddington," Trace said.

"He's dead."

"When'd you find out?"

"When I read it in the paper last week," Bigot said.

"No inkling before that?"

"No."

"What'd you think about it?" Trace asked.

"I thought it was a shame."

"Why a shame?" Trace asked.

"Just a regular shame. You know, a guy dies before he should, it's a shame."

"Just a general all-purpose shame? Not a special-attachment personal shame?"

"No." Bigot seemed to sit up straighter and more of his torso came out of the water. Trace saw that his neck was crisscrossed with four different gold chains, two of them with some sort of medallions hanging from them.

"You were the Paddingtons' doctor?" Trace asked.

"Yes."

"How well'd you know them?"

"Well as anybody else around this town, I guess. Maybe even better. Hell, I guess better than anybody except the vet. He saw them all the time."

"What's the vet's name?"

"William Palmer. He died last year, so don't bother looking him up," Bigot said.

"He saw the Paddingtons a lot?"

"If you were a vet and you had patients—you know, I never know, do vets call the owners patients or the dogs patients?"

"Let's call them clients for identification," Trace said.

"Okay. You're a vet and you've got two clients

who own twenty-seven dogs, Jesus, I guess you're going to see a lot of them."

"So what kind of people were they, the Paddingtons?" Trace asked.

"Fill these up, will you?" Bigot took Nurse Teddy's champagne glass and held them forward to Trace. "There's a fresh bottle in the cooler there."

As Trace opened the bottle and poured wine, Bigot said, "They were the dullest couple in the world. If they didn't have money, no one would ever have noticed them."

"Why do you say that? What makes a couple dull?"

"Sitting around playing Scrabble at night," Bigot said.

"There's got to be more than that," Trace said. He handed Bigot one of the glasses. Nurse Teddy snaked up an arm to take her glass. Her right breast followed the arm out of the water and Trace thought it was a very nice right breast.

"First of all, Nadine was homely," Bigot said.

"A lot of women are homely, though."

"Not homely like she was homely," Bigot said. "I mean, those teeth, she could eat corn on the cob through a mail slot. Bad, man."

"Paddington wasn't bad-looking, though," Trace said. "I saw his picture."

"No, Hemmie was all right. But he was funny. He was poor and hardworking and then he made a lot of money and he was one of those guys who, well, it wasn't so much that he didn't know how to enjoy being rich, it was more like he never even realized he was rich. You know, there are people like that."

"I'm not one of them," Trace said. "When I'm rich, I'll know it."

"See, that's what I mean. You'd know it and I'd know it," Bigot said. "But not Hemmie. I mean, come on, even his nickname. Hemmie? That's a wimp nickname. If I had his money, my nickname would be Pad. Or Heller. Or Lee. Something, not Hemmie."

"He couldn't have been all that dull," Trace said.

"He was. Trust me, he was. Like he thought all that bullshit about the sperm whale and stuff was on the level. He thought that all those entertainers who get involved in crap like that, he thought they were legit. He didn't even know that they did all that crap for publicity."

"You think they do?" Trace asked.

"What do you think? Remember that guy, I don't remember his name, I think he's dead, he played in that television series about a racist, like a funny series. And the worse of a racist the character became, the more stupid left-wing organizations he joined."

"Why was that, do you think?" Trace asked.

"He didn't believe any of that left-wing crap, you can count on that," Bigot said. "What it was was that he was feeling guilty 'cause he was making ten million dollars or something, and he was afraid that people in Hollywood might think he was like his character. They're all pansies in Hollywood. Remember that series, Teddy?"

"No. I never watched it, I don't think," she said.

"Oh. What were we talking about?" Bigot asked Trace.

"We were talking about Paddington thinking all these pansy Hollywood phonies were on the level," Trace said. "Mind if I have some of that wine?"

"Help yourself. No, Hemmie didn't understand things like that. That's why he didn't have any fun or anything."

"You ever tell him that?" Trace said.

"Sure. A lot of times."

"You were close? Play golf or something?" Trace asked.

"No, not like that. I didn't see Hemmie much, but when I did, I always told him what I thought."

"Where'd you see him?" Trace said.

"Mostly around here. Once in a while, he'd come over for his checkup or something . Nadine was always with him, but I kept her out of the examining room. Once in a while, I'd go over there for dinner. Not very often, though. I got it, you want to know how often I saw him."

"Right."

"Maybe every couple of weeks or something. He said I was his best friend. Can you believe that?"

"And you weren't?"

"He was a jerk," Bigot said.

"Not that much of a jerk, maybe. I mean, he was doing the Hollywood routine, wasn't he?" Trace said.

Bigot laughed hard and started to choke on his champagne. Nurse Teddy ministered to him by pounding his back.

"What'd you hear about that?" Bigot finally said.

"A couple of newspaper clippings that he was doing the big-money number in Hollywood. Starlets, yabbadabbadoo, the whole thing."

"What bullshit," Bigot said.

"I saw it in black and white. Would a supermarket newspaper lie to me?" Trace said. He noticed that Nurse Teddy had never taken her eyes off him, not even when she was pounding on Bigot's hairy back. He smiled at her.

"Here's what that was all about," Bigot said.

"Tell me about it," Trace said.

"What a joke. I was going out to Las Vegas for a break, and Hemmie and Nadine were in Los Angeles. I didn't have any luck at the tables, so I went up there to meet them and I hung around for a couple of days. I had some business anyway. Once in a while, Nadine would have a meeting of the Guppy League or something that Hemmie didn't go to, so I'd take him out to dinner. And I made sure that we always had a couple of booby traps around."

"Booby traps?" Trace said.

"You know. Twiff. Actress types, and I kept duking the restaurant people to take pictures and then just print Hemmie and the woman next to him, and then I gave them to my press agent and told him to try to get Hemmie some ink."

"Wait a minute. *Your* press agent?"

"Right. Nev McBride, the best in the business. I don't have him anymore."

"If you don't mind my asking, what's a doctor doing with a press agent?"

"Hey, medicine's all bullshit. The difference is in the packaging. I was thinking that maybe I'd move to California, Beverly Hills, that kind of thing, and I wanted to make sure that the right crowd would recognize me. So I hired Nev."

"I see. What happened?"

"Nev got Hemmie a couple of mentions. You know, he made up some bullshit about financing pictures or whatever, but that was all crap, nobody who listened to Hemmie for a minute would believe that. I had to work extra hard at being charming to keep the twiff awake during dinner 'cause all Hemmie would talk about was some freaking animal, some mountain goat or something."

"And then what?" Trace asked.

"Then we came back home. And when the clippings came, I made sure Hemmie saw them." Bigot said. "I mailed them to him." He grinned slyly. "Anonymously." He had large yellowed teeth with spaces between them.

"Did Mrs. Paddington see them?"

"She did. Do you know they opened each other's mail? Can you believe that? So the clippings came and she saw them."

"I bet he caught hell," Trace said.

"Maybe. He called me on the phone and said it was all very embarrassing and it was hard to explain to Nadine. But, hey, she had to believe him, didn't she, that it was all harmless. I mean, what the hell, where else could she go with those teeth?"

"I don't know," Trace said. "Some women murder their husbands for things like that."

"Naaaah, not them," Bigot said. "It'd take more than that."

"You sure about that?" Trace said.

"They were lovebirds, I tell you."

"What'd you do it for?" Trace asked.

"Do what?"

"The whole thing, starlets, press agents, all of it?"

Bigot shrugged a big hairy-shouldered shrug. "It was fun. I thought it'd be fun. Give them something to worry about. Who knows, Hemmie might want to get into producing movies."

"You ever talk to him about that?"

"Yeah, but he wasn't really interested. Too bad too 'cause I had good friends through Nev and there were some good properties available for the right kind of money. But Hemmie . . . naaah, he was a stick in the dirt."

"When'd you see Paddington after that, after the clippings appeared?" Trace asked.

"I been thinking about that," Bigot said, "and actually I guess I didn't see him anymore after that."

"It wasn't too much later that he was killed," Trace said.

"I know. I read about that in the paper and I tried to remember whatever day it was that he got killed, but I couldn't. Around here one day is pretty much like another. Deadbeat people. Dead-ass and deadbeat."

"So you don't know if anything special happened around the time he disappeared?" Trace asked.

"Like I said, no. You remember anything, Teddy?"

"No," the blond woman said.

"Did you talk to Mrs. Paddington around that time?" Trace asked Bigot.

"No, I didn't talk to her at all."

"Maybe she was mad about those Hollywood clippings?" Trace suggested.

Bigot paused as if considering that for the very first time. "I don't know," he said. "I can't understand why she should be. It was just for fun."

"You examined Paddington for the insurance policy," Trace said. "How was his health?"

"He was fine. Nothing wrong with him, except he had a little . . . what's the word?" He looked helplessly at Teddy.

"Chronic," the woman said.

"Little chronic cough," Bigot said, "but nothing except that."

"What caused the cough?" Trace said.

"I don't know. Some people cough. Don't you worry about it. He was as healthy as a horse." He chuckled. "As healthy as one of their dogs. Both of them were."

"You treated Mrs. Paddington too?"

"She didn't need treatment. I checked her once in a while, every year or so, but she was fine."

"She's not so well now," Trace said.

"What's the matter?" Bigot asked.

"I don't know. She's old-looking and tired. Grief, I guess. She's got pinkeye."

"There's a lot of that going around," Bigot said. "But I never saw her eyes. I didn't see much except her teeth. I'm getting crowns. Real crowns. Six hundred dollars a crown it's going to cost."

"Is that a lot?" Trace asked.

"Well, you can get them done around here for two-fifty a crown, but I'm going to have them done in Beverly Hills."

"A lot of money."

"Another client of Nev's. He's giving me a break, but you get what you pay for, I always say."

"You ever hear from Mrs. Paddington's doctor in Westport?"

"What's his name?" Bigot asked.

"I thought you might know. You might have sent records or something."

"Not me," Bigot said. He looked at Teddy. "Anybody ask you for records?"

Nurse Teddy was looking off into the distance and apparently had not heard the question.

"Hey, wake up," Bigot said. "Anybody ask you for Nadine's medical records?"

"No, honey," she said.

"No. I guess the answer is no."

Nurse Teddy was looking at Trace. She said, "Does Mrs. Paddington have pinkeye now?"

Trace shrugged. "I don't know. A couple of days ago, she said she had a touch of it. Why?"

"I don't know. I was just wondering," Teddy said.

Trace waited, but she offered nothing to fill the ensuing silence and Trace asked, "The Paddingtons have any other friends that you know about?"

"No. They were hermits, like I said. Did I say that? I think I did. They were hermits."

There was something biting and coarse about

Bigot's speech and Trace said, "Where are you from?"

"Not French, if that's what you mean. I mean, French ancestry but not from France or like that. I don't talk French at all."

"Except champagne," Teddy said. "He can say champagne."

"And *al dente*," Bigot said.

"That's good," Trace said. "People on the Italian-French border will be very impressed. No, I meant where in the States are you from?"

"Hoboken," Bigot said.

"Pretty far from Hollywood," Trace said.

"Hey, it wasn't too far for Frank, was it? Frank made it, and when I was growing up, I thought, Hey, if that no-talent string bean can make it to Hollywood, why can't I? I mean, hell, I sing better than he does. And I'm a *doctor*."

"The crooning medic. You've still got a good shot at it if that's what you want," Trace said.

"No. Beverly Hills, that's for me. Plastic surgery, no night calls, nobody dying on you. Do eyes and noses. Around here, you're always getting women, they say there's something wrong with their gallbladder and they need medicine. You know what they need," he said, and punched his fist into the air in a sexual gesture. "That's what they need. No more of that. California. You know my house is California-style?"

"I noticed," Trace said.

"They hate it around here, these narrow-minded bastards, but I don't care. I think it's great," Bigot said.

"It is, it's a great house," Trace said, "but I can understand how the natives might get restless. I don't imagine they'd think much of your house *or* your life-style."

"Exactly. You'd be amazed at how they hate me," Bigot said. "They take everything out on me, but the hell with them, I'm going to do what I want."

The look on Nurse Teddy's face as she looked at Dr. Bigot was one of unalloyed admiration. Trace thought, I guess that's what they mean when they say personal taste makes horse races. Suddenly, Trace thought there was something sad about it all and he wanted to get out of there.

He rose from the sling deck chair he had been lounging in and said, "Do you know who the Paddingtons' lawyer was in town?"

"Sure. Ben Johnson. He represents everybody in town who can afford his outrageous fees. A goddamn country lawyer, and he charges like he's in Hollywood. I think it's a hell of a world where a lawyer can make more than a doctor, right? All lawyers do is make misery, and us doctors, well, you know, we cure and heal, you know, like that. You think they understand that in this town, though?"

"Some people just don't know what's good for them," Trace said.

"That's the truth," Bigot said. "I'm going to practice in Beverly Hills for a while and then I think I'm going to go into the restaurant business. A nice elegant place, where I don't have to put up with a lot of people's bullshit. Just come in once a week, pick up the receipts, maybe hang around and say hello to some people, sing a song or two, maybe a duet with Frank, and leave."

"You'd quit your medical practice?"

"You can make a lot of money in Beverly Hills, but it costs a lot too," Bigot said. "You've got to have fancy supplies, buy a lot of things, those little wood things for sticking down your throat, and those . . . What do you call them, little knives?"

"Scalpels," Nurse Teddy said.

"Right, scalpels. There's a lot of stuff like that. Restaurants are easier."

"Be careful," Trace said.

"Why's that?"

"Seventy-five percent of all new restaurants fail," Trace said.

"That's only for jerks who don't know what they're doing, put in money when they don't know anything about it. You won't find me doing that."

"Wise man," Trace said. "You'd be surprised how many people fall into that trap."

"Jerks. All of them," Bigot said. "Not us. Not me and Teddy." Trace saw the doctor move his hand under the water to stroke Nurse Teddy's leg.

"I think I'll be on my way," Trace said.

"Before you go, would you open us another bottle of champagne? It's Major André, but it's real good. A lot of people don't know how good it is, spend a lot of money for fancy stuff with some big fancy dumb name that nobody can pronounce, like Don Pigeon, but I like André."

Trace opened another bottle from the wooden ice chest, handed it to Bigot, and said, "Well, thanks for your time. I really appreciate it."

"Lock the gate on your way out. I don't want anybody else barging in back here."

"Sure," Trace said. He had just turned the corner of the house when Bigot called his name. He turned around.

"Yeah?" Trace said, looking at the hairy doctor and the beautiful blond nurse in the California hot tub in New Hampshire, drinking Major André champagne.

"We're married, you know," Bigot said.

Trace looked blank.

"Teddy and me. We've been married for four years."

"That's nice," Trace said. He didn't know what he was expected to say.

"But don't tell anybody; it's nobody's business," Bigot said.

"I won't," Trace said and walked away again, thinking, How sad. How terribly sad.

The sign outside the white frame house said, BENJAMIN Y. JOHNSON, J.D. ATTORNEY AT LAW. Johnson was a tall weed-thin man in his sixties. Everything about him was thin, Trace thought. His hair was white and thin, slicked back against his head. His lips were thin, almost nothing but lines bordering the opening of his mouth. He wore thin wire-framed glasses. He was wearing a three-piece suit, his shirt collar heavily starched and buttoned tightly, even though there was no air-conditioning in his office and the place felt like a steam bath.

If this man had been his high-school science teacher, Trace would have hated him. But if he had had to hire a lawyer, he'd look for someone like Johnson: mean, humorless, get down to business, let's do it and get it over with, and screw the enemy any way we can.

Johnson looked through his wire-framed glasses at Trace's business card, as if examining a rare bug on the end of a pin. Most people gave the card back when they finished looking at it. Johnson put it inside a small parquet box atop his large, highly polished oak desk.

"So what can I do for you, Mr. Tracy?" he said. His voice was thin too. It reminded Trace of Henry Fonda playing Abraham Lincoln.

"I'm looking into the death of Helmsley Paddington," Trace said.

Johnson's face remained as impassive as if he had not heard Trace.

"You know, of course, that he's dead," Trace said.

"I read in the press of his purported death," Johnson said.

"Purported? Why purported, if you don't mind my asking?" Trace said.

"From what I read, his body has not been found. No court has yet made an official declaration of his death, so until then it is purported. When a court of valid jurisdiction says that Mr. Paddington is dead, then it will no longer be purported; it will be a fact and I will refer to the fact of his death."

Get me out of here, Trace thought. The man's not human. The next thing, his eyes are going to start rotating, he'll paralyze me with a glance, and spirit me off to the Planet Nitpick and put me in a zoo.

"Yes, very well," Trace said. He cleared his throat. "Were you a friend of Mr. Paddington?"

Johnson thought for a moment as if weighing the possibilities.

Finally, he said, "No. I wouldn't say so. He and Mrs. Paddington were occasional clients when they lived here."

"Would you mind telling me what they were occasional clients for?" Trace asked.

"Why are you asking these questions?" Johnson asked. "Just what is it you are 'looking into?' "

"Before my insurance company pays Mrs. Paddington's death claim, we want to make sure there is no fraud involved." Trace paused. "It's not only the money. We would hate to see someone hoodwink a court by falsifying information."

Johnson considered that noble aim. Finally, he laced his thin fingers together and said, "Very well. I will help you, as long as I don't think that answering in any way affects client-attorney confidentiality."

"Thank you," Trace said.

"You asked on what I represented the Paddingtons. It was a minor business matter of whether or not they should create a corporation to handle their ownership of stock in a large British corporation. I told them, no, that, in my opinion, a corporation would be of no real economic or legal value to them."

"Did you discuss this with them in person?" Trace said.

Johnson looked slightly surprised at the question. "Yes," he said. "They came to this office and we discussed it here."

"Did you ever socialize with Mr. and Mrs. Paddington?"

"What do you mean by socialize?"

"Go to dinner together. Meet at the club.

Belong to the same civic groups where your paths crossed, that sort of thing," Trace said.

"No."

Trace felt again as if he were asking questions of a person being paid not to respond. Johnson seemed to notice the look on his face, because he said, "I regret, Mr. Tracy, that I cannot be of more help. Mr. and Mrs. Paddington were very reclusive by nature. I do not think they had any real friends in this town or anywhere else. They seemed quite content with each other's company."

"I know this is a tough question, Counselor, but do you think their marriage was a good one?" Trace asked, and because he knew the question that would follow from Johnson, he added, "By good, I mean a loving, caring, faithful marriage."

"I have no firsthand knowledge of that," Johnson said.

"Your impression, sir, as a worldly-wise man."

"I would suppose that, yes, they did have such a marriage."

"I was told that Mrs. Paddington may have thought that her husband had been fooling around with motion-picture actresses," Trace said.

"May I ask where you heard that?" Johnson said.

"From Dr. Bigot. He was the Paddingtons' physician."

The first glimmer of emotion showed on Johnson's face. His eyes narrowed, and if he were a gunfighter, Trace knew he would have drawn and fired at that moment.

"Dr. Bigot is an idiot," Johnson said.

"I know what you mean," Trace said. "California life-style, blond nurse, that kind of thing."

"I mean that the man is an idiot. I don't care at all about his life-style. He is a certifiable idiot who had to go to medical school in Guiana. He should not be permitted to practice. He knows less about medicine than I do."

"He told me that a lot of people in this town didn't like him," Trace said leadingly.

"Did he tell you that he is under indictment?" Johnson asked.

"No," Trace said.

"Very well. There are many retired persons in this area. Dr. Bigot began a service specializing in the treatment of the retired, those on Social Security pension. It all sounded very good except that he billed for services he did not perform, and for tests he did not administer, and several patients found they had serious illnesses after Bigot assured them they had none. He has been indicted for fraud and his medical license is under review."

"I didn't know that," Trace said.

"I would not imagine that he had told you that," Johnson said.

"No, he didn't. Basically, all he said was that

he was the Paddingtons' only real friend in town."

"Friend? That man has no friends. By friendship, I would imagine that he meant he was always nosing around the Paddingtons trying to get them to invest money in some scheme or other."

"He said he wants to open a restaurant," Trace said.

"Seventy-five percent of all new restaurants fail," Johnson said.

"I know."

"In the case of any that Dr. Bigot is associated with, you may raise that figure to one hundred percent," Johnson said.

There was a pause for silence and Johnson said, "Is there anything else, Mr. Tracy?"

"Just one thing. Did you handle the sale of the Paddington house here when Mrs. Paddington moved?"

Johnson thought silently for a moment, then spun his chair around and removed a file from a cabinet behind him. As he leafed through it, he said, "I don't believe that the house was sold, Mr. Tracy. I believe it was only rented. Yes, here it is."

He was holding a letter typewritten on a small sheet of ivory-colored stationery. Stapled to it was a larger piece of onionskin paper with typing on it and the red word "Copy" printed across it.

Johnson began to read.

" 'Dear Mr. Johnson, Could you please recommend the name of a real-estate agent who might be able to handle the rental of our home? We are considering leaving West Hampstead for a while. Thank you. Mrs. Helmsley Paddington.' " He flipped the paper and said, "And I recommended they contact Mr. Barton McNick. He is a local realtor."

"She never told you why she was planning to move?" Trace said.

"We did not communicate except by these two letters," Johnson said.

"Her letter is pretty formal, isn't it?" Trace asked.

Johnson looked at it again and finally did something human. He shrugged. "I don't know," he said. "It seems clear enough. Considering moving, looking for a real-estate man to rent their house. Do you think Nadine should have included a recipe for apple turnovers?"

"I guess not," Trace said. "Can I find this Barton McNick in town?"

"One block south from here," Johnson said.

"Thank you for your time, sir," Trace said.

"You're very welcome," Johnson said. He had spun again in his chair to return the Paddington file to the cabinet.

At the door, Trace stopped and asked, "Mr. Johnson, why do you dislike Dr. Bigot so?"

Johnson looked surprised that such a question need be asked. "Because he is an incompetent, sir."

"Is that the only reason?" Trace persisted.

"Need there be any other?" Johnson said.

"I guess not," Trace said.

Barton McNick was a medium-sized man whose pear-shaped body seemed designed by nature and ordained by gravity to sit in a chair. All the while he talked to Trace, he ate with both hands from a large salad-sized bowl of salted peanuts. Trace moved his chair back an extra foot, which he figured was just outside the effective spray range of peanut chips. When one landed in his lap, he moved the chair back another foot.

"There's a house on Eugene Road," Trace said. "I was wondering if it's for sale or rent."

"What's it look like?" McNick asked.

"Big English Tudor house, fenced grounds, couple of acres, looks like it's got kennels alongside it."

"That's the Paddington place," McNick said. He took time out to chew and swallow. "Too bad. That place is already rented out."

"Oh, damn," Trace said.

"I've got some other good stuff just like that to look at," McNick said.

"Stay with this one house for a minute. What'd you call it, the Paddington house?"

"Right."

"Why's it called that?"

"Those were the people who used to live there. They still own it. The Paddingtons. They were big into dog food or something. That's why the kennels."

"They moved from that beautiful house?" Trace said.

"Yeah. About seven, eight years, I guess."

"And you've been renting it since then?"

"That's right. Why you so interested in that house?" McNick asked.

"Because it's my dream house. For Lola and me and little Ernie and Benjie. Benjie's our dog. He's a surly mistrustful paranoid little cur, but we love him. We've always looked for a house just like that. Tell me. Just a rough idea. What's a house like that worth around here?"

"Three hundred thousand, I guess. Or you mean rental?"

"I mean rental," Trace said.

"They're paying twenty-two hundred a month plus utilities," McNick said. For the first time, he broke the symmetrical poetry of his motion. He had been eating peanuts from his two hands alternately. Now he grabbed two handfuls and tried to push both into his mouth at once. A lot of them dribbled on the desk. He picked them up and popped them into his mouth and smiled sheepishly at Trace. "I skipped breakfast and lunch today. I'm dieting."

"I've heard good things about the Peanut Diet," Trace said.

"Well, it's not really a diet. These are just a snack until I eat dinner," McNick said.

"The tenants at the Paddington house, they have a long lease or something?"

"No, they just rent month to month, but they've been there a couple of years now."

"Do you think that house might come available in the future?"

"Maybe. Would you be interested in just renting or possibly buying?" McNick asked.

"Would the owners sell?"

"I think they still want to rent."

"Wouldn't it make more sense to sell?" Trace said. "I mean, if it's gone up, it's a big capital gain, right?"

"Sure. But the woman, I don't think she wants to sell."

"Did you ask her?" Trace said.

"I wrote her a couple of letters. Every so often somebody says that maybe they'd like to buy it, and I write her a letter and she writes back and says, No, just keep renting it."

"Where does she live? Would it help if I called her?"

"In Connecticut, but you couldn't get through. Like I just heard that her husband died, this woman's, and I called to ask her if she wanted to sell, but I couldn't get through."

"No answer?" Trace said.

"No, this Mrs. Paddington has these two people that work for her, they used to work for her up here too. This redhead with beautiful knockers. I talked to her. She said Mrs. Paddington wasn't feeling good but just keep renting the house."

"What do you do with the rent money, if you don't mind my asking?" Trace said.

"I just mail it to Mrs. Paddington, after I deduct my fees for management," McNick said.

"Well, listen, I'm sorry that house isn't available now," Trace said. "I'm just passing through, but I'd really be interested in any property you have to offer."

"That's why we're here," McNick said, peanuts flying.

"So would you put me on your mailing list? For everything. And commercial property too. I might be interested in opening a restaurant around here."

"Restaurants are always good," McNick said. "A good investment."

"I know that. Take my card," Trace said. He shuffled in the back of his wallet for a business card. "Send me everything you've got on different properties."

McNick looked at the card. "Walter Marks," he said.

"That's right. I'm the vice-president of that company."

"Sure thing, Mr. Marks. I'll keep you posted on everything."

"Good. And if you get anything really special, give me a call, will you?" He took the business card and wrote Walter Marks' phone number on the back of it.

"That's my home number," he said. "Call me with anything good."

"Sure. Any best time to call?"

Trace thought a moment, then said, "I'm sorry about this, but I do most of my work at home at night. You know, from midnight till eight A.M. Could you possibly call me after midnight?"

"Sure. No problem."

"Thank you," Trace said. "You're very kind."

13

Trace got back to the Westport motel after eleven P.M. He had stopped along the highway a couple of times for drinks and had bought a bottle of vodka because he didn't want to spend the night in his room without a drink.

He thought, fleetingly, that he might be drinking too much. "But," he said aloud in the car as he drove, "how much is too much?" For a child or a person who couldn't handle it, even one drink might be too much. Yet there were people in the world who drank vast amounts and stayed sober and in good health. In some places in Russia, they drank vodka every day and lived to be 912 years old. At least. He had seen it on a yogurt commercial, and yogurt commercials never lied. So that was that. Trace decided that he drank just enough, and he was very glad that this current "just enough" was so much more than the "just enough" of the past few months when he was drinking virtually nothing but wine and hating every sip of it.

When he was rich, as soon he must be, no one would ever again tell him how much he should drink.

Two messages had been slipped under the door of his room; he picked them up and lay them side by side on his bed and poured himself a drink. Vodka, neat. No ice. No mixer. Just a plastic tumbler of liquor with nothing to spoil it. Then he looked at the two messages.

One read, "Call Chico." The other read, "Please call E.L.V."

Chico. He understood that message. "Call Chico." Clear and simple. But "Please call E.L.V." What was that all about? First of all, he knew no E.L.V. Second, he knew no one whose message to him would be preceded by "Please." Who could this E.L.V. be who dared say please to him?

Maybe someone he had befriended many years ago? He lay on the bed with his drink in hand and looked at the message. That could be. Maybe someone he had done a favor for years before, someone who had now come into a lot of money and wanted to share their good fortune with Trace. He'd have to think about that some more.

He called Chico after first looking up their telephone number on the back of a matchbook

cover he kept in his wallet. That was another
thing wrong with the world. Matchbook covers.
He had once spent three months perfecting his
big trick: opening a matchbook with one hand,
folding down a match, closing the book, and
striking the match, all with the one hand. It
was a wonderful trick to use when driving,
particularly when your cigarette lighter didn't
work, and his never did, or when you were
driving in Texas, where everybody wanted to
smash head-on into your car and you needed to
keep both eyes on the road. It was a real good
trick and then some Naderian idiot had decided
that the world was in danger of incineration
because the striking pad on matchbooks was on
the front of the matchbook and they had put
the pad on the back of the book. And his trick
was rendered obsolete. His one trick. Why didn't
the busybodies of the world stick to toxic waste
and wheels that fell off cars, and leave the important things, like matchbooks, alone? If they
wanted to warn America about something, why
didn't they warn it about the Mexicans? Didn't
they know that the Mexicans had won both
gold medals in walking at the Olympic Games?
If sleeping ever became an Olympic event, the
Mexicans were going to be a real danger to U.S.
sports supremacy. Why didn't they worry about
things like that?

If they needed something to keep them busy,

why not find out who E.L.V. was and make him stop bothering people?

Chico annoyed him just by answering the telephone. Her voice was light and airy and happy, the way it always was. Just by saying hello, she could disgust an ordinary person who knew that the world was a mean and sour place. What was wrong with the woman? Didn't she know that a telephone call could be a harbinger of disaster?

Hello, indeed. I'm calling to tell you that you have an incurable illness. Hello. This is the IRS. We want all your money and we're impounding your sixty-five pairs of shoes until we get it. Hello. This is the Berlitz school; your Japanese mother has finally decided to learn to speak English and she has driven three instructors crazy and we're suing, and we're calling you because your mother says she is not desponsible and why are we horrowing her?

"Hello" was all Chico said.

"This is Trace."

"Drunk again, I see," Chico said.

"That isn't quite correct. If I were really drunk, I wouldn't have called. Yet, here I am, calling. I am not drunk. Q.E.D."

"You sound drunk."

"A serious throat malady," Trace said. "One for which the cure is very expensive and I just can't afford it. I drink to numb the pain."

"I'm sorry for your troubles," Chico said.

"But not sorry enough," Trace said.

"Exactly. Not sorry enough," she agreed.

"Why did you call?" Trace asked.

"That so-called friend of yours from New Jersey, what's his name, Eddie?"

"Yeah?"

"He called," she said.

"What'd he want?"

"He said he got new repair estimates on the restaurant. There was more damage than he thought. Your share of the repairs is eighteen thousand dollars. He needs it right away," Chico said.

"Eighteen thousand? That thief."

"That's what I told him," Chico said.

"What'd you tell him?"

"I told him he was a thief," she said.

"What'd you go and do that for?" Trace said.

"Because he's a thief and you're not likely to tell him and I thought somebody should."

"Madam. Unless you are willing to invest in this golden opportunity, I think you should refrain from calling the general partners names."

"I feel better for having done it, and no, I'm not investing in that beached whale. Why are you drinking so much?"

"I feel better for it," Trace said.

"You were doing reasonably well with the wine," Chico said.

"It's job-related stress. It has forced me back to hard liquor."

"Exercise is good for stress. Much better than alcohol," Chico said.

"I tried exercising for you. I even bought running shoes. And what did it get me?"

"You ran once around the dining-room table. You did one push-up three times a day. For two days. That's not really an exercise program."

"You have to start somewhere," Trace said. "I'm thinking of going back to it. What are you doing?"

"I'm dieting and exercising."

"You exercise every day," Trace said.

"I'm exercising more now," she said.

"Why are you dieting?" Trace said.

"I gained three pounds and it's got to come off."

Trace said, "I gained three pounds today between twelve and one."

"That's you, not me. I'm dieting."

"I think you should only diet on high-protein flesh sticks," Trace said.

"You're a sex maniac," she said.

"True. So true," Trace agreed. "So are you going to lend me the money or not?"

"Not," she said.

"Well, then, this is probably it for us," Trace said.

"I'm really sorry about that," she said.

"If I shouldn't call again, remember . . . well, remember that I only wanted the best for you."

"I will," Chico promised. "Good night."

"Wait a minute," Trace said.

"What?"

"Do I know anybody named E.L.V.?"

"E.L.V.?" Chico said. "I don't know. Why?"

"Somebody called and left those initials," Trace said.

"Man or woman?"

"I don't know. I forgot to ask."

"Probably some woman you've picked up in the last couple of days. That broad you bopped the other night when you were mad at me."

"I'm still mad at you," he said. He was thinking that Chico was right. E.L.V. stood for Elvira. She hadn't wanted to leave her name, so she left the code initials. Good thinking, Elvira.

"You'll sleep it off," Chico said.

"Not this time," Trace said.

"Good night," Chico said.

"Good-bye forever," Trace said.

He hung up the telephone. He didn't want to call Elvira. He didn't want to call anybody. All he wanted to do was to feel sorry for himself.

It was midnight.

14

Trace's Log: Devlin Tracy in the Paddington matter, three A.M. Thursday, two more tapes in the master file.

Well, this is it, folks. My very last report in my very last case in my very last day on earth. I've finally found the solution to my problems, courtesy of a Jesuit professor in college who told me once that suicide represented a drastic attempt to improve one's life condition.

It's the only way I have left.

What, you may ask, brought me to this low point? And all I can answer is mathematics.

For instance, I never knew the meaning of geometric progression until I heard Eddie's reports on storm damage and what it'll cost to swab out a cellar. Ten thousand, twelve thousand, fourteen thousand, eighteen thousand. Every day I don't pay is another day that the water puddles sit in the cellar, festering, and the bill goes up.

And I've got no chance of getting the money, no chance at all. Chico won't lend it to me, Sarge doesn't have it, my mother won't lend it to me because my name's not Bruce. My ex-wife didn't respond to my telepathic messages to send me a check. The loan sharks would put electric drills into my kneecaps if I borrow and can't pay back. I'm done. Doomed to a life of poverty, all my savings gone, my hopes for the future vanished in a puff. But before I live poor, I'm taking the pipe.

I harbored some slim hope that I might be able to find out something in this Paddington case that might get me a fat fee, but that hope is gone. I tried everything. Walter Marks, damn his pelt, wouldn't bite when I tried to let him think I was being bribed by Mrs. Paddington. How did he know? If I were the vice-president for claims of an insurance company, I would sure as hell have a more open mind than that. But, no, not Groucho.

So, world, how did I spend my last day on earth? I spent it, most of it anyway, with Alphonse Bigot, late of Hoboken, soon of Hollywood. And, of course, his platinum-blond wife, Teddy.

Just thinking about him makes me even sadder. Here's a guy under indictment for defrauding the elderly, and he thinks the town hates him because he sings better than Frank Sinatra. He wants to be a Hollywood swinger so much he can taste it and he's forced to resort to sitting in a hot tub in New Hampshire with his wife, drinking Major André champagne.

Sad. But all men are sad who have hair on their shoulders. Why do men who have hair on their shoulders and backs never have any on their heads? Is there a certain amount of hair juice in your body, and if you waste it all on your back and shoulders, your head gets starved? The gorilla component. Maybe everybody's got a certain gorilla component. Some use it for back and shoulders. Others, the civilized decent ones like me, spend most of it on their heads. This is a scientific point I would check out if I were going to continue living. If we could understand the gorilla component, we could predict baldness early. Then we could hustle the suckers with all kinds of things. Shoulder and Back Hair Retardant. Call it Fur No More. Make hair grow on your head, where it's supposed to, instead.

I should mention this to someone to look into. Ah, well, forget it. It's just another one in a long string of real good ideas that I had and the world ignored. Now that I've decided on suicide, it makes me no never-mind.

I am leaving all this data for whom it may concern so that old Gone Fishing knows I did

189

my best. Please make a copy of this tape and send it to Chico so she knows how she hurt and destroyed me in the final painful moments of my life. If you decide to cremate my body, please make sure I'm wearing my underwear.

If I ramble a little, it's because I want to leave this permanent record of my thoughts in the hope that they will help someone else later on. Just call it building a bridge for those who will come after me.

So I thought I had a chance of proving that Mrs. Paddington killed her husband because he was catting around on her, but then I met Dr. Alphonse Bigot of the Medical School of Guiana and Beverly Hills. And he blew away my last hope.

Bigot knew the Paddingtons, not real well, but at least better than anybody else in town. And he set up all that Hollywood-starlet crap, just as a joke, just to get Paddington into trouble with his wife.

That's what he told me, and I believe him because he didn't have any reason to lie to me. Probably he could tell he was talking to a dying man.

But he didn't know anything about Paddington's death, and Paddington had a chronic cough but nothing else, and he was in good health and so was Nadine and she didn't have pinkeye, and he didn't know who their Westport doctor was. Ooops, *her* Westport doctor; Hemmie was dead before the move.

A doctor with a Hollywood press agent. I do, I truly do want to die.

And this silly-looking Band-Aid on my face when I got punched and all this tape on my ribs don't help either. I hurt. My body hurts and my spirit hurts even more.

I can't wait to get out of here. Bigot was my last chance and he wasn't any help at all.

Lawyer Benjamin Johnson was no more help. "Purported death." What a pain in the ass he was. I couldn't even bring myself to ask him if he thought that Nadine might have killed her husband. He wouldn't have known anything. They weren't friends, not real friends anyway, I guess, and when Nadine wanted to move, all she did was write to him.

And real-estate man Barton McNick just collects the checks and sends the money to Mrs. Paddington, and he thinks that Nadine doesn't want to sell.

Groucho, if you get any advertisements for houses in New Hampshire or any late-night calls about good restaurant deals, it's just my little gift to you. Barton McNick handles good stuff and I thought it might be perfect for you to look into.

So that's it. If anybody takes this case after me—and I don't know why anybody should 'cause there's nothing here—anyway, this is what I would do.

I would check into Nadine's financial status in Westport, her mortgage, stuff like that. I don't know why, but I would. I think I would go talk to the cops to see if they know anything. I would go make love to Elvira.

How fitting it is, Chico. You abandoned me in my moment of need and my last thoughts on earth were of making love to somebody else. I hope you carry that shame with you for a long time.

Oh, a final thing. Chico, please take care of this for me. I forgot my expenses the day before yesterday, and while I didn't leave the room that much, I had a lot of food sent in, so that was ninety-five dollars, including tips for the delivery boys. Add another fifty for miscellaneous. That's one-forty-five. And yesterday or today, whatever, I went up to New Hampshire and I drove and ate on the road and made a lot of phone calls and all kinds of stuff like that, and so it was at least two hundred and fifty dollars, so make it three hundred. So that's four-forty-five for the two days.

Chico, please make sure you collect this money from Garrison Fidelity. I want you to use it to endow a special college fund to help lift the burden of making a living from big thinkers, so they have time to pursue their dreams. Jus make sure that nobody who owns a restaurant ever gets a penny of it.

Well, I guess this is it. The end of everything. I feel as if I should make a big complicated speech in leaving this earth, but I don't have one in me. I have been hurt too many times in my life, but I forgive you all. Remember that, folks. Remember that, Chico. The last thing I did was to forgive you.

On my tombstone, I just want my name engraved. Well, maybe you could add a small line or two. Nothing fancy or pretentious. Just something simple. Maybe "Here lies Devlin Tracy where savage indignation can no longer rend his mighty heart." Write it in Latin.

Take care of that, Chico. Thank you very much.

Hoping all your news is good news, this is Devlin Tracy saying good night and good-bye forever.

15

Trace filled his glass with vodka and drank that. Then he did it again. Then he saw the bottle was empty and he thought it was a hell of a way to die, wanting a drink.

So he decided not to kill himself and went to sleep. Tomorrow was another day.

16

He wished he was dead when the telephone rang, loud, insistent, squawking, next to his ear.

"Hello."

"Hello, Trace. This is Elvira. You didn't call."

"Who?"

"How quickly they forget. Elvira."

"Oh, sure. Sorry. You woke me up. I got in late," Trace said.

"And when did you go to sleep?" she asked.

"Huh?"

"Never mind. You *are* groggy. You want me to wait while you light a cigarette or something?"

"My something's all empty. I finished it last night. You talk, I'll light a cigarette," Trace said.

"I missed you yesterday," Elvira said.

Trace was silent as he lit his cigarette. He

hated possessive women. Was she going to try to become one on the basis of one tumble? Didn't she know how close he had been to death the night before? Didn't she care?

But now Elvira was silent too, so finally Trace mumbled "Uhuh" in agreement.

"But I thought about you all day," she said brightly. "I was working for you."

"How's that?" Trace asked.

"I kept an eye on the place across the street all day. I didn't take my eyes off it for a minute."

"And?"

"And nobody went in or out all day. Not a soul."

"Somehow I don't think that's the big breakthrough I need," Trace said.

"I saw the woman, what's her name?"

"Mrs. Paddington?" Trace said.

"No, the other one. Maggie. And the man working around the garage."

"Maggie Winters and Ferdinand," Trace said.

"Right. They were working around the garage most of the day." She paused for comment.

"That's real good," Trace said.

"That doesn't help at all, does it?"

"I can't think of how, right this minute," Trace admitted.

"Hell, I was trying to be helpful."

"I know." Why had she called him? Trace wondered.

"Do you know why I was trying to be helpful?"

"You believe in truth, justice, and the American way?"

"Because I wanted you to come over here and sleep with me last night," Elvira said.

"I'm sorry. I had to go out of town and I was real late getting back."

"You're in town now. Come over today."

"I've got some stops to make today," Trace said.

"Can't they wait?"

"They're kind of important, actually," Trace said.

"Can I help? God, I'm begging you. Do you realize that? You're not even handsome and I'm begging you. Why is that?"

"Because you know I'm a good person," Trace said. "Maybe you can help. You know anybody at the local bank? Or the town real-estate office?"

"Probably. I have to think about it," Elvira said. "Why?"

"I'd like to know about the house across the street. Who owns it? What the mortgage is? Do they pay on time? Like that."

"That's a tall order," Elvira said.

"If it were easy, anyone could do it," Trace said.

"I'll try. Will you call me later?"

"Yes, I will. I promise," Trace said.

"You make sure," Elvira said as she hung up.

Trace finished his cigarette while deciding whether to throw up or not. He was annoyed that his butt can had been removed again by the maid. But there was something nice about starting the day talking to a woman so crazed for your body that she pleaded. All he needed now was for some other crazed woman to call, so crazed that she would lend him money, something on a sliding scale from ten thousand to eighteen thousand dollars, depending on how crazed she was. For eighteen thousand dollars, he would perform the Hindu rope trick in bed. Without a rope. For ten thousand, he wouldn't. He had his pride.

He smoked three more cigarettes, stubbing them out in the midget ashtray, waiting, but nobody called to offer him money. He got up, greatly annoyed, and in the bathroom found out that he didn't have to throw up anymore either. If that was the kind of day it was going to be, he might just as well stay in bed.

He couldn't remember when he had eaten last. It was a good thing to eat every so often, especially when you reached forty. Every doctor would tell you that. And you should have fiber in your diet. That's why he ate Fish-Doodles at bars while having a drink. He really liked cashews better, but it was a rare bar that put out cashews. The best he ever really hoped for was salted peanuts and smoked-sausage sticks.

Maybe his life was meant to be cursed.

Maybe there would never be a moment he could put his head down to rest. Maybe there would never be anyone who could share the burdens and the glory with him.

It certainly hadn't been Jaws, his ex-wife. He had figured that out in the earlier days of their marriage. He had been working as an accountant and he had rented a summer shore cottage for Jaws, What's-his-name and the girl, his two kids.

One night, after a particularly tedious day of double-entry bookkeeping, he had stopped for a few drinks on his way from work to the shore. Women just didn't understand pressure.

He went into the bungalow, lay on the couch, and fell instantly asleep. Jaws seemed to think this was intended to be an insult aimed at her cooking. She tried to wake him up to eat. He grumbled that he was tired. He could always eat, but he had to sleep now.

"You don't like my cooking," she had said.

Trace had mumbled, "You're the only woman I ever saw who needed Helper Helper in the kitchen."

He had gone back to sleep. They were alone in the bungalow. What's-his-name and the girl were out firing crosses on people's lawns or something.

He must have been snoring a little bit. He always did when he lay on his back. Later, his wife said that his snoring really annoyed her. So she went out the rear door of the bungalow, which was right on the beach, and brought in a Styrofoam cup filled with dry sand.

Then while he lay on his back, mouth open, snoring, she poured sand down his throat.

No one who has never had sand poured down his throat would ever understand. He coughed, choked, and sputtered. He washed it out finally with water, left the house and washed away his hurts with vodka, and decided then and there that his marriage was doomed.

It took years before he could afford the divorce settlement, but as soon as he could, he left. The cost was pretty steep because his lawyer refused to state in court that What's-his-name and the girl weren't Trace's children, and that they were fathered by person or persons unknown or were the results of spontaneous conception. Even after Trace had sent him an article from a science magazine that said a thirteen-year-old virgin in Peru had given birth to twins.

Trace wondered what people paid lawyers for anyway. All lawyers were perfectly willing to lie and cheat and steal for themselves, but when it came to their clients, they all turned into George Washington near the cherry tree.

After his shower, Trace taped his small recorder to his right side over his kidney. Then he dressed, carefully threading the wire that led to the golden-frog microphone through his shirt, before attaching it to his tie. He found the clipping file Walter Marks had sent him in a dresser drawer and looked through it until he found

he report of the private detective, C. S. Brunner.
Attached to his report was the list of people he
had spoken to, and Trace found the name he
had been looking for.

"Lt. Sam Roscoe, please," Trace said.

"Who are you?" The uniformed clerk in po-
ce headquarters was pleasant. Public servants
n towns like Westport were always polite, be-
ause they never knew that the person they
were talking to wasn't the president of a televi-
ion network.

"Roone Arledge," Trace mumbled. The sun
ad made his head throb and his ribs hurt un-
er the tape. Maybe suicide had been the right
dea, after all.

"Sorry, sir, I didn't catch your name."

"Devlin Tracy." Trace handed him a business
ard. The policeman looked at it, and when he
aw it didn't have anything to do with Holly-
vood or television, he said gruffly, "Sit down
ver there, please. I'll see if the lieutenant's free."

The office where Trace waited was plastered
ith no-smoking signs. Westport was a quiche-
ater's paradise, he thought. He lit a cigarette
nd flicked the ashes in an old Styrofoam
offeecup that the police department's maid ser-
ice obviously had overlooked.

Lt. Sam Roscoe was a two-cigarette wait and
en Trace was nodded into a back office by the
niformed clerk.

Roscoe's office was small but seemed a
brightly lighted as the Los Angeles Coliseur
for a night baseball game. There were two sepa
rate overhead fixtures, two floor lamps, and
desk lamp. All were turned on. Roscoe was
short lean man with handsome hawklike fea
tures. His mouth was thin-lipped but seeme
always on the verge of smiling, as if he ha
noticed something funny where others had no
The suit he wore was very expensive. Trac
knew that because he owned very expensiv
suits too. The difference was that it looked lik
an expensive suit on Lt. Roscoe; on Trace a
suits looked like junk and Chico had once a
cused him of stealing all his clothes from
Volunteers of America collection container.

"Tracy?" Roscoe said.

"Yes."

"Sit down. What can I do for you?"

The real leather chairs in the detective's offi
were cushioned and soft, much like Roscoe
voice, which oozed confidence and poise.

"I'm in town looking into an insurance claim
Trace said. "I always like to check in with tl
police so you know I'm around."

"What claim?" Roscoe said. He was sittii
behind his desk, looking at a long roll of pap
that had come from a Teletype machine.

"It's complicated, but it involves a fami
named Paddington. According to the wife, the—

"I know about the Paddingtons," Roscoe sai

"Your company had detectives looking into that a month ago. Why you now?"

"The detectives didn't find out anything. I'm the last best hope for saving my company two million dollars."

"Are you any good?" Roscoe asked.

"Not really," Trace said. "But I'm real lucky."

"That's the only way to win a lottery," Roscoe said.

"And sometimes the only way to figure out an insurance fraud," Trace said.

"You think there's a fraud involved?" Roscoe asked.

"I don't know. I've got a boss who always thinks that, so he sent me for one last look around. You said you know about the Paddingtons. If you don't mind my asking, how come?"

"How'd you get my name?" the police officer said.

"I ran across it in the report the p.i. did for the insurance company," Trace said.

"Well, the p.i. working on it was my brother-in-law, C.S. So I knew what he was up to." He paused a moment, then swiveled his desk lamp so that it shone on Trace's face. He inspected Trace's bruises for a moment at long distance, then said, "What's the other guy look like?"

"Like King Kong," Trace said. "I guess you told your brother-in-law everything you might know about the Paddingtons."

"Everything, which was zero," Roscoe said.

"No little hints of scandal, no calls to the police at four A.M. about screaming from their place, none of that?"

"Nothing. I told C.S. you wouldn't even know the Paddingtons live in town," Roscoe said.

"Technically, they don't, I guess," Trace said. "Only one of them lives in town. The other one is dead."

"Pay the money. I don't think you're going to find out anything. You're wasting your time."

"I figure that too," Trace said. "But I don't have any choice."

"Why not?"

"See, I invested in this restaurant and now, even before it gets open, it's got storm damage and I've got to come up with my share of money to fix it."

"Only people who own restaurants should invest in restaurants," Roscoe said.

"You're going to tell me that seventy-five percent of all new restaurants fail, aren't you?" Trace asked.

"No. Is that true?"

"It certainly is," Trace said. "Three-quarters of them go down the toilet."

"Then why'd you invest?" Roscoe asked.

" 'Cause I'm as thick as shit," Trace said.

"Not too many guys know that."

"About me or about themselves?" Trace asked.

"Everybody knows it about me."

"About themselves. Who worked over your face like that?"

"I don't know. I got jumped in a parking lot."

"In town?"

"Yes," Trace said. "The other night."

"No idea who did it?" Roscoe asked.

"An idea, but not a fact," Trace said.

"If you turn it into a fact, you let me know," Roscoe said. "There are laws against that kind of thing." He glanced back down at the Teletype sheets on his desk, as if there were something important there that he wanted to get back to.

"I'll get out of your hair in a minute, Lieutenant," Trace said.

"No, don't worry. It's just that I get all the jobs that nobody else does," Roscoe said. "Missing persons, fraud, stolen cars. I spend all day reading reports from all over. What do you want from me?"

"Did you ever meet Mrs. Paddington?"

"No. But I talked to her once."

"How was that?" Trace asked.

"I was trying to help my brother-in-law a little, so I drove up to the Paddingtons' house. The maid was there, the pretty one."

Trace nodded.

"She told me that Mrs. Paddington was under sedation and that she'd get back to me. And she called me that afternoon and I asked her a couple of questions and didn't get any good answers, but I gave it all to C.S. for his report," Roscoe said.

"Do you like your brother-in-law?" Trace asked.

"Who likes his brother-in-law?"

"I was just wondering," Trace said.

"I can't stand him," Roscoe said. "If I had any brains myself, before I got married I would have looked at him and said, 'That is my wife's gene pool. Stay away from these people.' But I didn't. He is dumb and borrows money and doesn't pay it back."

"But you wouldn't want his business to fail, would you?"

"Christ, no. He'd probably move in with me. What are you getting at?"

"Sorry, Lieutenant. I just had to satisfy myself that you weren't holding back on me because you were afraid I'd show up your brother-in-law."

"I'm not," Roscoe said.

"I just want you to know I don't work that way. If I found out there was something going on here, I'd make sure that C.S. got some of the credit. As long as I got the fee."

"That's big of you, but not necessary," Roscoe said. "I told you what I know."

"Then, thanks a lot, Lieutenant." Trace got up to leave and Roscoe said, "You staying around town long?"

"Ye Olde English Motel. A couple of days."

"Where do you live?"

"Las Vegas," Trace said.

"You *are* lucky," Roscoe said.

"Sometimes," Trace said. "Sometimes."

Trace was hungry, so he walked from police headquarters to a restaurant on the corner. It was much too bright and filled with plants.

He asked the hostess for a table away from the plants.

"Why?" she asked.

"Because I don't trust them. They suck up my carbon dioxide before I'm done with it."

She sat him in the back with a bemused look and a menu. As she walked away, he told her, "If Paul Newman comes in, tell him I'm busy and want to be left alone."

He hoped that Newman and Robert Redford wouldn't come in. He hated being pestered when he ate and he knew that Newman would start insisting on making everybody's salad dressing and Redford would go from table to table, begging money to save Montana or something. The last thing he needed today were more pests.

He picked at a cheddar cheeseburger, had a couple of drinks, paid his bill, and telephoned Elvira. He had no driving sex urge now, but he believed in planning ahead. If the urge didn't show up, he'd pretend he had a headache and back out.

Elvira's voice on the telephone sounded as if she were talking on a shortwave radio. He asked her about it and she said that she was talking on the radiophone from her front yard.

He thought of her in her tiny bikini and was very glad he had called.

"Are you coming over?" she asked.

"Am I invited?"

"I'm waiting for you."

"Good. I'll be right there," he said.

"And I've got big news to report," she said.

"What's that?"

"Come over and I'll whisper it in your ear. Vodka all right?"

"Sounds good to me."

Elvira was in place on her beach towel, her breasts bigger, her legs more sweepingly lush, her smile even more dazzling than Trace had remembered.

She lifted her face to be kissed. He leaned over and brushed her lips lightly.

"That's a pretty poor excuse for a kiss," she said.

"The neighbors. I don't want to ruin your reputation."

"I love it when you're thoughtful. Let's go inside and fuck."

"You already poured me a drink. Mind if I sample it?"

"Go ahead. You'll pay for it later," she said. "I found out about the mortgage across the street. Hey, what happened to your face?"

Trace sipped at the drink in the lawn holder. It was still vodka and Kool-Aid. "I walked into a husband," he said. "What about their house?"

"Mrs. Paddington bought the house seven years ago. It was two hundred thousand dollars. She put down forty thousand. Her monthly mortgage including taxes is nineteen hundred dollars. She's never been late on a payment."

"The house is in her name?" Trace said.

"Right."

"How'd you find all that out?"

"I've got a friend at the bank," she said. "He told me."

"That was real good," Trace said. "That was your big news?"

"Oh. No. They went out." She pointed in the direction of the Paddington house.

"Who did?"

"All of them, I guess. I saw the big goon and the peasant girl. Mrs. Paddington must have been in the backseat. They were using that Mercedes with the smoked windows, so I couldn't see too well."

"When was this?"

"About an hour and a half ago or so," Elvira said.

"You see anything else? Anything unusual?" Trace asked.

"I saw a picnic basket. The woman, Maggie Winters, she had one of those big Styrofoam coolers and she put it in the trunk and then she put a picnic basket there too."

"If you were a gambling person, would you say they were going on a picnic?" Trace asked.

"I'd give odds," Elvira said.

"How long does it take to go on a picnic?" Trace asked.

"When you take a car, it takes you to get there and to get back and all the time it takes you to eat potato salad."

"Couple of hours, right?"

"Sure."

Trace got to his feet. "I'll be back in a little while," he said.

"Where are you going?"

"To look around." He saw the small cordless telephone on the large teddy-bear towel, next to Elvira's feet.

"Listen," he said. "I'm going to call you in a couple of minutes with the Paddingtons' phone number."

"Breathe heavy at me. I love it," she said.

"No. I want you to stay here, and if you see their car coming back, I want you to call me quick. Ring twice and hang up. Then dial again. Ring twice and hang up."

"And you'll know enough to split, right?" Elvira said.

"You catch on real quick," he said.

"I want you to know you'll pay for this."

"How's that?" Trace asked.

"I'm not used to taking second place to a burglary."

"I'll see if I can steal you something nice," Trace said.

The gate was locked with a chain, but on the south side of the Paddington property, Trace found two bent bars in the high spike-topped fence and was able to slide between them.

He ran to the garage and found the door unlocked. He slipped inside and closed the door behind him. The interior of the garage was bright and airy from a bank of windows that ran along the entire back wall. The red Saab station wagon was parked in one of the two car berths.

A door on the side of the garage was unlocked and led to a screened breezeway that separated the garage from the house itself. He tried the house door but it was locked. Through the window, Trace saw the kitchen. It had the look that kitchens always had when people were out of the house. There were no coffeecups on tables, no pots on the stove. He hoped there were no burglar alarms on the door.

The door seemed to be one of those with the lock built into the doorknob. Trace craned his neck against the window but could see no interior deadbolt lock on the door.

In movies now, it would be easy. A credit card slipped into the door and it would pop open. But he had tried that three times in his life with a net result of three scratched and broken credit cards. He went back into the garage and found a toolbox on a shelf over a worktable. From inside the box, he took a small paint scraper and a hammer.

He glanced through the screening toward the front gate. No signs of life.

He slid the paint scraper behind the molding that ran down the frame along the outer edge of the door. As usual it was held only by small finishing nails. It took only a few sliding moves of the paint scraper and the molding came loose. That exposed the lock housing and Trace used the edge of the paint scraper to reach in under the bolt and muscle it back just enough so that the door swung open.

He replaced the door molding before doing anything else. He used his handkerchief to muffle the sound of the hammer tapping the thin nails back into the frame of the door. When he was done, he replaced both tools in the box in the garage.

He walked into the kitchen and stood quietly inside listening. Elvira hadn't seen Mrs. Paddington in the rear of the car, so she might still be in the house. He heard no sounds. He closed and locked the door behind him and walked to the kitchen telephone and called Elvira.

"Yes?" she said.

"Here's the number."

"God, this is exciting," she said.

"If you see anybody, remember, ring—"

"Ring twice, hang up, call again, ring twice, hang up. I got it," Elvira said. "Will you hurry back here? Committing a crime always makes me horny."

"Hold that thought," he said.

Trace hung up and then moved the lever alongside the phone so that the ring was at its loudest. If Elvira called, he should be able to hear the phone ringing anywhere in the house. He hoped.

He glanced through the window. Still no one at the gate.

This is the way all degradation starts, he thought. One little breaking and entry. And then it would lead inexorably to spitting on the sidewalk, then smoking on a bus, and before he knew it, he would be creasing IBM cards and referring to women as "girls."

Even the biggest plunge started with one little misstep. Idi Amin probably started out by neglecting to spit-shine his army shoes.

Trace walked softly down the hallway from the kitchen, quietly opening doors as he went. Just off the kitchen was a bedroom large enough to be an apartment. It was lived in and the closets along one wall held men's clothes, the closets along the other women's.

He picked up a black-and-white photograph from the large dresser. It showed Ferdinand in a dark suit, looking exactly like an ugly moose in a dark suit. Standing next to him was Maggie. Her hair was darker when the picture was taken, but she was a notable beauty by anyone's standards, only a few inches shorter than Ferdinand and with the long silky body of a ballerina. With knockers.

What she might see in Ferdinand was beyond Trace. He had long since matured enough that he didn't question why rich and powerful men so often had beautiful women on their arms. But Ferdinand? A handyman, ugly and probably broke?

Who knew what went through women's heads? He certainly didn't.

He opened the drawer of a night table next to the large queen-sized bed, but there was nothing in it except cigarettes—mentholated True Greens—and women's lacy handkerchiefs and a toothpaste-shaped tube that bore no marking.

Trace opened the cap. The substance inside was a light green but had no odor. He took his cigarettes from his pocket and removed the cellophane from the pack. Into it, he squeezed a long strand of the green waxy substance, then recapped the tube and replaced it in the dresser drawer. He folded the cellophane neatly and put it into his inside jacket pocket.

The other rooms along the first-floor corridor were a sewing room, a room used as an auxiliary pantry, and a small guest room, with a bed stripped clean.

The drawing room, where he had interviewed Mrs. Paddington, and a large, formal living and dining room completed the first floor.

The wheelchair was again where it had been the first time he had been there, folded up, and again Trace stumbled against it. He wiped the dust from his hands on his trousers, then went to a front window and glanced out. There was still no sign of anyone at the gate, but he didn't know how much he trusted Elvira to keep her eyes open. She might decide to go inside to make another bathtub full of drinks, or she might work on the tan of her eyelids, or she might decide to seduce passing schoolchildren, and not pay any attention to Mrs. Paddington and her two servants returning home.

He padded lightly up the steps to the second floor. There were three guest bedrooms, two baths, and a master bedroom with its own bath.

All the rooms were empty. He looked around in the master bedroom. It was a chintzed, breezy big room, bright and sunny. A large dresser stood in the corner near the window. He opened it drawer by drawer. Four drawers were empty; the top two contained women's underwear, slips and stockings, in styles that Trace felt could most charitably be called practical.

The night tables were empty. Not even a book or a magazine inside. The walk-in closet was filled with women's clothes, all of them with plastic dust shields over the hangers.

He looked inside the medicine cabinet in the bathroom. All it held was a plastic bottle of aspirins and a small half-empty bottle of Natural-tone Makeup for Oily Skin.

Trace came back out and looked through the drawers of a desk that sat by the front window. All he found was some blank writing paper and a pen. The writing paper was in a neat stack.

Trace heard the telephone ring downstairs. It rang twice and stopped. He looked through a window and saw Ferd unlocking the front gate. The gray Mercedes was stopped behind him, with Maggie at the wheel.

The telephone rang twice again. Trace closed the desk drawers and ran downstairs.

He heard the car approaching up the stone driveway. He let himself out through the kitchen door onto the breezeway. He heard the sound of protesting machinery as the garage door opened, probably from an electronic buzzer inside the car.

He darted out through the back door of the breezeway and crept along beneath the garage windows.

The car pulled in and the door lowered itself again. He heard the car's motor die as it was turned off. He heard two voices, a man's and a woman's, but he couldn't make out the words.

He carefully raised his body toward the corner of one of the windows and peered inside. He saw Ferdinand and Maggie going through the door to the breezeway. Ferd had his hand familiarly on Maggie's rear end. Trace ran toward the fence on the garage side of the house.

Moving behind bushes, he found his way to

the bent bars of the fence, let himself out into the wooded field next door, and then walked quickly to the road.

Three minutes later, he was sitting on the grass next to Elvira, sipping a fresh drink.

"I thought you'd be ready for one," she said. "That was a close call."

"Sure was. Thanks for the help."

"Did you find anything?"

"Not a blessed thing."

"What did you hope to find?" she asked.

"I don't know. A confession that Mrs. Paddington killed her husband or something. But whatever it was, it wasn't there."

"Too bad."

"I don't know. It's good practice keeping my burglary skills in order. Thanks again for helping."

"I expect more than thanks," Elvira said as she slithered toward him across the large teddy-bear towel.

17

Trace was at the bar of the Ye Olde English Motel cocktail lounge. The need for ten to eighteen thousand dollars was still heavy on his mind and he was making a list of all the money he could put his hands on, including all the people who would definitely lend him money.

It was not a particularly long list. He had about four hundred dollars in his checking account. He had another five hundred in a cashier's deposit box at the Araby Casino. He figured that he would be able to beat Garrison Fidelity out of seven hundred dollars on the Paddington investigation. That totaled sixteen hundred dollars.

In a separate column marked loans, he had listed his father as the big investor at five hundred dollars. Somehow, Sarge could come up with five hundred dollars. Trace had written his mother's name, but then had drawn a line through it.

Eight bartenders were listed for a hundred dollars each and six waitresses for fifty each. One blond hatcheck girl who worked at an Italian restaurant near the Desert Inn was down for two hundred dollars. So were two pit bosses at the Araby Casino. The concierge at his condominium building was good for one hundred and so was the woman who cleaned their apartment three times a week. Another nineteen hundred dollars.

He decided not to include on the list Cora, his ex-wife, whose last words to him had been "I hope you melt in a nuclear accident," and his mother, whose last words to him were, unfortunately, never the last.

He doubted if his kids, What's-his-name and the girl, had any money. If they did, he doubted that they would lend it to him. He was sure that Tugboat Annie had poisoned their minds against him, just because of pettiness, just because he didn't do sappy sentimental things like visit them or write them or call them. Women were ungrateful wretches, he thought, which brought him to the most ungrateful wretch of all. Chico.

They had been together now for four years, and on a scale of zero to ten, those years were evens. This wasn't a low mark, Trace thought, because he could not remember another year in his life that was higher than a three, which meant that he could have spent most years entirely in bed and not have missed a thing worth remembering.

Trace added up the list. Three thousand five hundred dollars. It wasn't that he didn't have friends, he realized. He had lots of friends. His trouble was that none of his friends had any money. All his friends were bartenders or waitresses or degenerate gamblers. The rare insurance-company president, who might have had real money, was a drunk and he wasn't good for anything.

He did some calculation. He was anywhere between sixty-five hundred and fourteen thousand five hundred short of what he needed.

Chico could make up the difference with a sweep of her magic pen and magic checkbook. He ordered another Finlandia by pointing to his empty glass. Of course. Chico would have to make up his shortfall. That was that. They had been together too many years now and she owed him.

A voice inside him whispered, She doesn't want to invest in a restaurant. She's afraid of losing her savings.

There's no way to lose here, Trace told the voice.

She doesn't believe that, the voice said.

Stop throwing obstacles in my path, Trace responded. She will lend me the money.

Be realistic, the voice insisted.

All right, Trace conceded. Maybe she won't lend me all the money, but she'll lend me a lot of it.

Put her down on the list, then. But be realistic, the voice cautioned.

Trace wrote the name "Chico" down on his list. He paused for a long time, the ballpoint pen stolen from the lawyer's office poised over the paper.

Realistic? Realistic would be that she would acknowledge her gratitude to him for dragging her naked out of a hallway and lend him all the money he needed.

He sighed and marked her down for one hundred dollars.

The woman had no character; she belonged working in a geisha house.

He drank his vodka and crumpled the napkin into a lump and dropped it into the ashtray. Life sucked.

Two messages had been slipped under the door of his room. One read "Call Walter Marks." Trace threw that one away. He didn't want to talk to a man who wouldn't lend him money. The other read, "Please call E.L.V."

Again? Was the woman insatiable? Didn't she realize that if he spent all his time in bed, he

221

would have no time for drinking or for commerce?

It was time to end this romance before she got too dependent on him, he decided. He dialed her number. After a week of rejection, it might feel good to reject someone else for a change.

"Hello, Elvira. Listen, I . . . I want you to know—"

"Trace, they had a visitor across the street," the woman interrupted.

"Oh? Who?"

"I don't know. I didn't see him real good. It was some guy with dark hair. I was in the house and I just glanced out and saw him and Ferdinand at the gate. Then about a half-hour later, I saw two cars come out."

"His car?"

"Yeah. A red Mercedes convertible and the station wagon."

"See who was driving?" Trace asked.

"No. It was too dark for that. Is this good stuff I'm getting for you or what?"

"Real good," Trace said.

"Listen, Trace, there's something else."

"What's that ?"

"I won't be able to see you anymore. My husband will be home tomorrow."

"That's a fine how-do-you-do," Trace said. "You're dropping me like a hot potato?"

"Well, when my husband's home. You going to be around next week?"

"No, I don't think so."

"Then I guess this is good-bye," Elvira said.

"I guess so," Trace said sullenly.

18

Trace's Log: Devlin Tracy in the matter of Helmsley Paddington, only one tape in the master file, and it's midnight Thursday.

This is the day I was going to kill myself, but I talked myself out of it. Moral to be drawn from that: always, always, do whatever pops into your mind. First impressions are always best, and I would be better off dead.

But I'm not. I spent one more day in this vale of tears looking at the Paddington claim, and I'm finished. I even committed burglary and didn't get anywhere. Tomorrow I'm going back to Las Vegas. It's easier to commit suicide in Las Vegas. Just drive out into the desert until you run out of gas and then walk in the sun until the heat fries your brains and the vultures swoop down and pluck out your eyeballs. Like Prometheus. It's the only way to go.

If anybody is listening to this drivel, this is what the day was like.

I went to see Lt. Sam Roscoe at the Westport police and he didn't know anything either about the Paddingtons. His brother-in-law was the private eye that Groucho hired to look into this case; Groucho was overcharged, but the report was accurate. Nothing funny happened to Helmsley Paddington.

Roscoe talked to Mrs. P. on the phone and didn't get anything that made him suspicious, so that's that. What can I do that a smart cop can't do? Anyway, Roscoe was interested in how I got my bruises. Maybe I'll tell him that I got them from Ferdinand who cold-cocked me in a parking lot. That might do the trick.

The only good thing that happened to me today was that Newman and Redford didn't bother me while I ate lunch. Elvira checked with some old boyfriend at the bank and there was truly nothing big to notice about the Paddington mortgage. Nadine bought the house, paid forty thou, owes one-sixty, and is on time with the monthly payments. Big deal.

Ferdie and Maggie went on a picnic. Well, why not? They sleep together. Maybe they're married? I never thought of that. You know, world, I never thought of a lot of things. I should have checked to find out if Ferd and

225

Maggie have police records. I don't even know Ferd's last name. Well, that just goes to show you. Even the smartest brains in the world can go on hold when they're overloaded with other problems, like finding money to fix a restaurant.

Mrs. Paddington, I guess, went with them on the picnic because she wasn't in the house when I broke in. But I didn't see her when they came back either. I mean, they just walked into the house, goosing each other, and if she was in the backseat of the Mercedes, they were just going to let her stay there. And her dusty old wheelchair was still under the stairway in the house.

I don't know, maybe they lock her in the cellar when they go out. Maybe she's the Prisoner of Zenda.

So, anyway, I break into the house but I don't find anything except a picture of Maggie before she bleached her hair and Ferd looking like newlyweds. Maybe they *are* married.

But nothing else. In Maggie's room, I got this tube of green waxy stuff that's here in my pocket. I don't know what it is, but it's probably something real important like aloe vera hair-conditioner.

And there wasn't a thing in Mrs. Paddington's room. Dusty clothes but nothing else. Not even a book in the nightstand. It's all right to be sick, but jeez, you don't have to be dull about it. Mrs. Paddington's got to be the dullest woman in the world. You'd never know she was in that room.

So then I had to go pay off Elvira for being such a good detective's assistant and later she dumped me, so that tells you what a great lover I am. And I figured out every place in the world where I could get money, and the most I can raise is thirty-five hundred and that's counting on Chico for a hundred, and I don't think I could get it from her.

Oh, and somebody visited the Paddington house tonight but Elvira didn't know who, except he had dark hair and a red Mercedes convertible.

Who cares?

I don't.

I'm going to go to sleep and tomorrow I'm leaving this burg. Christ, I was in a bar today and I saw somebody order Pimm's Cup. I ought to figure out my expenses tonight but I'm too tired even to cheat.

I'll do it tomorrow. And then I'm going home to Las Vegas and I'm going to drink and drink and drink until I can't think about my troubles anymore and they have to come and send me to the place with the rubber room.

This is some end for a guy who was voted second-most-likable person in his junior-high-school class.

19

Basically all he wanted to do when he went to bed was sleep. Why couldn't the world understand that simple thing? If it wasn't women who wanted to jump his bones, it was something else, like the phone always ringing. Leave me alone, world, Trace thought as he struggled to consciousness. I'm turning off and tuning out.

But the phone wouldn't stop and he finally picked it up and snarled, "Pleasant middle of the evening to you."

"Mr. Tracy?" a woman's voice asked.

"Now, who else would it be?" Trace said.

"I don't know if you remember me. This is Teddy Bigot. Dr. Bigot, remember?"

"Oh. Right. Right."

"Has my husband contacted you?" she asked.

Trace started to come awake. "No," he said. "Was he supposed to?"

"Well, I don't know. I heard him say that he was going to talk to you. I think that's what he said." Her voice was halting and slow.

"Why don't you ask *him*?" Trace suggested. "I'll hold on."

There was a pause that was a beat too long. "He went on a trip. I haven't heard from him yet. I'm sorry to bother you, Mr. Tracy. I just wanted to know if you'd heard from him."

"Wait a minute," Trace said. "About what?"

"Doctor doesn't tell me what's on his mind too much," she said as she hung up the telephone.

"Then Doctor's a shmuck," Trace yelled into the dead telephone.

He thought about going back to sleep but saw sunlight peeking from under the tightly closed drapes. He opened them a crack and brightness assaulted his eyes like English darts. He closed the blinds again and looked around for his watch. It was after ten A.M. He had slept later than he expected. He steeled his nerves, gritted his teeth, and opened the blinds again. Then he went into the bathroom to throw up and shower down.

Then he sat on the bed. He was going to return to Las Vegas, that was for sure. But what was that stupidness with Teddy Bigot? What was that all about? That she had been

229

nervous and lying was obvious. But why? About what?

He got the Bigots' number from information and called her back. He would apologize for being groggy; he would ask her what he should tell Dr. Bigot if he should hear from him. He would twist her around and break through her facade and find out what was really on her mind.

There was no answer.

Well, that was that. Good-bye, Westport. Good-bye, Mrs. Paddington.

"Hello, Lieutenant."

Sam Roscoe looked up from the watercooler.

"Tracy, right?" Trace nodded, and Roscoe said, "Come on inside." Trace followed the policeman into his sun-bright office and Roscoe said, "What's new? You find whatever his name is, Paddington hiding out in an old mining camp?"

"Afraid not," Trace said. "I didn't find out anything, so I just came in to tell you I'm going home. I like to check in and check out."

"I didn't think there was anything to find. My brother-in-law looked pretty hard, and even if he is a dumb shit, he probably would have bumped into something if it had been there."

"I couldn't either," Trace said. "I guess it wasn't a good season for dumb shits."

"So what's next? Your company pays up? Is that the way it goes?"

"I don't know," Trace said honestly. "I never really understood the insurance business." He shrugged. "I guess the court says that Paddington's dead and then we have to pay because there isn't any reason not to. The court says he's dead, he's dead and that's that. Two million dollars."

"Almost makes dying seem worthwhile, doesn't it?" Roscoe said.

"Hell, I'm dying for ten thousand dollars," Trace said.

"Why is that?"

"The restaurant deal I told you about. I'm going to cut my wrists."

"What a jerk. It *is* a bad season for dumb shits." Roscoe sat down and looked at the pile of Teletype messages in front of him. "Listen, if you decide to take the pipe, do it someplace else. I've got enough work to do. Missing persons, stolen cars . . . Christ, don't they ever stop?"

"A policeman's lot is not a happy one," Trace said.

"Spare me the Gilbert and Sullivan," Roscoe said without looking up from the sheets of paper.

"You don't have an Alphonse Bigot in that list, do you?" Trace said. "A doctor from New Hampshire?"

"Is he missing?" Roscoe said, looking up quickly.

"I don't know," Trace said.

"That question you just asked me, does it mean anything?" Roscoe said.

"I guess not," Trace said.

"Don't waste my time. Enjoy Las Vegas."

"Thanks for all your help, Lieutenant."

"Wasn't much," Roscoe mumbled. He was busy reading the reports again, and Trace left quietly.

Trace went back to his room to pack. He thought about calling Walter Marks but decided to wait until he was safely back in Las Vegas. There was never any hurry about delivering bad news.

"What are you doing here?" Trace asked as he pushed open the door to his room.

Chico looked up from the table near the window where she was sitting. Trace's tape recordings were spread out on the table in front of her and she had the earphone of the small recorder stuck into her ear.

She pulled the earphone out, turned off the tape recorder, and said, "Well, I'm glad to see you didn't commit suicide." Her smile was dazzling, but Trace didn't feel like being dazzled.

"You've been listening to my tapes," he sniveled. "You're not supposed to listen to my tapes. How many times do I have to tell you not to listen to my tapes?"

"Not even the one that was addressed to me posthumously?" Chico asked mildly. She scanned him up and down and said, "Your face still looks like hell."

"It's all your fault. I went to exercise class and I almost got killed in the parking lot and it's all your fault. Why'd you come here anyway? I'm going home."

"And leaving Elvira?" Chico said. "She must be a beauty."

"She is. She's a real beauty. And she would have lent me ten thousand dollars if she had it," Trace said.

"She told you that? I didn't hear it on the tape."

"Not exactly, but I can tell," Trace said. "I know good-hearted people when I see them."

"Particularly, I guess, when you see them real close up like you saw this Elvira. Was she good?" Chico asked.

"I'm ignoring that question. Watch me ignore it," Trace said. "How did you get in here anyway?"

"I have my ways," Chico said.

"Tell me about them. I always have trouble getting into places."

"Obviously you didn't have much trouble getting into Elvira's place."

"How'd you get in here?" Trace repeated with a disgusted look on his face.

"I waited for the maid to clean up and then I just breezed in like I belonged here. Maids never know who's supposed to be staying in a room."

"You're very devious," Trace said.

"But you knew that all along," Chico said.

"So what devious reason brought you here?" Trace said.

"I had a couple of days off. I thought you'd be glad to see me."

"I'm leaving."

"Why?" Chico asked.

"Because I'm not doing any good. I'm not finding out a thing. Pay the damned woman her damned money and let me go home and jump in Lake Mead."

"Sarge told me you sounded depressed," Chico said.

"You talked to him?"

"Of course. He's the only one in your family worth talking to. Present company included."

"You traveled twenty-five hundred miles to insult me?" Trace said.

"Oh, Trace, you're such a dork."

"Say what?"

"You're a dork. I came to make you rich," Chico said.

"You're going to lend me the money for the restaurant, right? I take back everything I said about you on tape."

"The postcard too. That I'm petty and mean-spirited and a small person?"

"Yes. All the other stuff too. Did you bring a check?" Trace asked.

"Better than that."

"You shouldn't travel with a lot of cash on you," Trace said. "Westport isn't safe."

"Better than cash."

Trace's eyes narrowed with suspicion. "Nothing's better than cash," he said. "What'd you bring?"

Chico held up the little cellophane package of green goo he had taken from Maggie's room the day before.

"You didn't bring that," Trace said. "I had that."

"You don't know what it is, do you?"

"No. What is it?"

"A solution to all your problems," she said.

He insisted that she explain herself and she did, and thirty minutes later when she had finished, Trace agreed. Yes, he was a dork.

The telephone rang even as Trace walked toward it. The caller was the man Trace wanted to talk to. Lt. Sam Roscoe.

The policeman said, "All right, Tracy, what's going on?"

"What do you mean?"

"The state police just pulled a car out of a quarry about forty miles north of here. A red Mercedes. It's registered to an Alphonse Bigot of West Hampstead, New Hampshire. He's the one you were asking about."

"That's right," Trace said. "Did they find his body yet?"

"No. Is he dead?"

"I'm afraid so," Trace said.

"I think you'd better get down here right away."

"We're on our way," Trace said.

20

The intercom buzzed on Adam Shapp's desk and he picked up the telephone, said, "Ask them to come in," and hung up.

"Mrs. Paddington's here," he said.

Trace nodded.

A moment later, the door to the office opened and the large bulk of Ferdinand loomed in the doorway. He was pushing Mrs. Paddington in the wheelchair.

Despite the heat of the summer day, she was dressed in a brown tweed suit, with man's-style walking shoes on her feet. She still wore dark glasses and the skin of her face was tan and looked leathery. Her pale hands were folded neatly in her lap. Trace looked at Chico, who nodded to him.

Ferdinand pushed the wheelchair into the

room and closed the door as Adam Shapp stood.

"Hello, Mrs. Paddington," he said.

"Hello, Mr. Shapp," she responded with her thick BBC accent.

Trace saw Ferdinand glaring at him and Trace winked. Shapp waved a hand toward Trace.

"You've met Mr. Tracy, I believe," he said.

"Yes, indeed," Mrs. Paddington said. "Hello, Mr. Tracy."

Trace stood up and smiled a long moment before answering. "Hello, Maggie," he said.

For a brief moment, the woman's face froze.

Then she said, "I beg your pardon?"

"I said, 'Hello, Maggie,' " Trace repeated. He saw Ferd's eyes dart from him to Shapp and back to Trace.

"Don't be upset and start rattling your chain, Ferd," said Trace soothingly. "It's all right. We know all about it."

"Mrs. Paddington," Ferd said, "I think you should leave this place. I don't like having this man around."

"That's a good idea, Ferdinand," The woman in the wheelchair said. "We should leave."

"You shouldn't leave yet," Trace said mildly. "Not before Dr. Bigot's wife arrives. I'm sure you'd have a lot to talk about with her. You could tell her about the quarry, Ferd. Where you dumped the car."

Ferd had been backing toward the door, pulling the wheelchair with him. He stopped suddenly now, his face hopelessly racked with confusion.

"We're leaving," he said, his voice soft and menacing. "Right now. Don't you try to stop us." He reached behind him to pull open the door, then took a step backward and bumped into Lt. Sam Roscoe, who had moved into the open doorway.

"I'm Lieutenant Roscoe of the Westport police," he said. "I think we should have a talk."

Trace moved forward in case Ferd should try to bowl over the smaller man, but Ferd just stopped. His shoulders drooped and he pushed the wheelchair back into the room. He looked down at the woman in the chair, who shook her head at him, sadly, then stood up and looked toward Trace and Chico.

"How did you figure it out?" she said. The British accent was gone.

"You made mistakes," Trace said, "and it wasn't meant to be. The Paddingtons might have been nuts but they were purebreds. You two are mutts. Especially Ferdinand. Once a mutt, always a mutt."

"That's not very complimentary," the woman said.

"It wasn't meant to be," Trace said.

"Damn it," Adam Shapp snapped. "This isn't Mrs. Paddington?"

"No," Trace said. "This is Maggie, her maid."

239

"Then where's Mrs. Paddington?" Shapp asked.

"She died in a plane crash," Trace said. "With her husband."

Trace and Chico were in the dining room of the Ye Olde English Motel. It was the first time Trace had seen it and it was a nice room, the kind he liked, with brick walls and not too many lights, but he was not happy, because when he had tried to order a drink, Chico had told the waitress, "He'll have a glass of rosé wine."

He felt like a boy kept after school for misbehaving. Sullenly he had ordered dinner, prepared to punish Chico by not eating any of it. But she hadn't seemed to mind, and when she had finished her dinner, she switched plates with him and started to eat his.

Sam Roscoe came into the dining room and sat at their table. He told the waitress, "Just coffee," and when she left, he told Trace and Chico, "It's a murder charge, too. The state police had divers all day at the quarry and they found Bigot's body. It looks like he was strangled."

"Too bad," Trace said. "He's never going to make it to Beverly Hills."

"Yeah, too bad," Chico agreed without lifting her head. Her mouth was full of food and she was talking while chewing. Barely had she swallowed when another load of supplies was heading mouthward.

"And Ferd's prints were all over Bigot's car," Roscoe said. "We got them coming and going. They're singing like birds now."

"Good," mumbled Chico.

"Evildoers take warning. If you want to steal quiche, don't do it in Westport," Trace said.

"You did a good job on this, Tracy," said Roscoe. He pushed back from the table as his coffee arrived.

"I couldn't have done it without the help of my loyal Eurasian assistant," Trace said.

Chico finally looked up. *"That's* for sure," she said.

"You know I'll have to take a statement from you," Roscoe said. "But that'll wait till tomorrow. I was just wondering what gave you the first tip?"

Trace looked blank, then said, "Chico, why don't you tell him about it? I don't like to brag."

Chico gulped down a final chip of breadstick and washed it down with a half-glass of milk that left a faint white mustache on her upper lip. Trace reached across the table to wipe it off with his napkin.

"Sure," she said. She turned to Roscoe and patted his hand and said, " 'Evening, Lieutenant. I'm sorry if I was rude, but I hate to talk when I'm eating."

"If that were true, you'd be silent most of the time," Trace said.

"Quiet. Or I'll have you explain it all to him," Chico said.

Trace sipped at his coffee. He wondered if he would be able to sneak into the bar after Chico went to sleep.

"There were hints all over the place," Chico told Roscoe. "First thing was that nobody ever saw Maggie and Mrs. Paddington together. You didn't, Lieutenant, and the lawyer didn't, and Trace didn't. When Trace went up there to see her, Ferd said that Maggie had gone to the store, but both cars were still in the garage and it's too far out to walk to town. That smelled fishy to anybody with any sense."

"It's easy for you to say," Trace grumbled, and Chico held up her hand for silence.

"So then Trace followed Maggie to the health spa and started pestering her. He's like that, a real pest. But he never gave her his name. Still, when he went downstairs to wait for her, Ferd bopped him."

"A sneak attack," Trace said.

"But the thing was, why did Maggie phone Ferd to come and meet her? Why didn't she just figure that Trace was your usual run-of-the-spa girl-chasing nerd. She wasn't supposed to know who he was, and the whole thing only made sense if she recognized him because she'd seen him while she was impersonating Mrs. Paddington."

"That makes sense," Roscoe said.

"Don't encourage her, Lieutenant. She gets very filled with herself at times like these."

"Can I tell him about the burglary, Trace?" Chico asked.

"What burglary?" Roscoe said sharply.

"It wasn't a burglary. I went up to the Paddington house one day and nobody answered, but the door was open so I went in looking to make sure that Mrs. Paddington was all right," Trace lied. "And I saw a couple of things."

"I don't believe that, but I'll make believe I do," Roscoe said.

"Anyway," Chico said, "Trace saw a whole lot of things. The wheelchair was still in the same place and it had a lot of dust on it. It hadn't been moved or used. And Trace didn't find anything in Mrs. Paddington's room. It's like nobody stayed there. There was a little bottle of makeup in the medicine cabinet. That was important."

"Why?" Roscoe said.

"Because it's a special makeup for oily skin. When I was a kid, I used to think I had oily skin, so I used it once. When it dried, I looked like the mummy in an old Hollywood movie. It wrinkles up your skin and makes it look old. Trace saw that about Mrs. Paddington right away, how young her hands were and how old her face looked. When they came to Shapp's office today, I could tell right away she was wearing makeup to look wrinkled. The hands were too young."

"Tell him about the green stuff," Trace said.

"Trace found this green stuff in a tube and didn't know what it was."

"What was it?" Roscoe asked.

"It was dental cement. I worked one summer in a dentist's office. It's what dentists use to stick temporary bridgework in place. Every time Trace looked at a picture of Mrs. Paddington or the one time he met her, and everybody he talked to, all anybody could think about was her big buckteeth. It was a terrific disguise. Maggie stuck in those phony teeth that she must have had made and nobody ever looked close at her."

Roscoe nodded. "She took them out when I was questioning her before. Said they hurt like hell."

"The hair color too," Chico said. "Trace saw a photo of Maggie and her hair was darker, and some real-estate guy in New Hampshire said she was a beautiful redhead. Why would a beautiful redhead decide to become a mousy blonde?"

"Some people like mousy blondes," Trace said. "Gentlemen prefer blondes."

"How would you know?" Chico said. "Anyway, she changed her hair color to match Mrs. Paddington's. She wore it long for herself and sprayed it up when she was playing Mrs. Paddington. Nobody in her right mind gets rid of beautiful red hair."

Roscoe nodded and signaled the waitress. "Another coffee," he said.

Trace was about to order a real drink when Chico said, "And another glass of wine for him." Trace turned around in his chair so he didn't have to look at the treacherous little Eurasian.

Roscoe said, "We tracked down Mrs. Bigot a couple of hours ago, and it's like you told me. When Trace was up there, he said that Mrs. Paddington had pinkeye. But Mrs. Bigot remembered that it was Maggie who had that when they lived up there. After Trace left, she mentioned it to her husband. He figured out that Maggie and Ferd were probably running an insurance scam. He had big money problems, so he went down to try to cut his way in."

"And Ferd killed him," Trace said.

"Well, they haven't admitted that part yet, but that's what it looks like. They killed him and then dumped car and body into that quarry. When Mrs. Bigot didn't hear from him, that's when she called Trace to see if he had heard anything. She got spooked when he said no, and she went to stay with relatives, but we tracked her down."

"Good," Trace said. "There was some other stuff too. When Maggie and Ferd wanted to rent that house in New Hampshire, she wrote to their lawyer, a cold, stiff kind of letter. It would have been so much easier just to telephone him. I figure that's because Maggie wasn't sure about what she was doing yet or if she could pull off the Mrs. Paddington impersonation."

Roscoe nodded. "She said that she was really scared about it for a while and that was the big reason they moved. So that no one would know them in a new town. But they were afraid to try to sell the house in New Hampshire because the bankers or somebody might recognize them, so they just rented it out and collected the rent checks."

"The biggest guess was the plane crash," Chico said. "Everybody Trace talked to said that the Paddingtons were always together. Even when he was in Hollywood, supposedly bouncing around with starlets, his wife was with him. It just didn't make sense that he'd go off to save seals or whatever it was without her. Did Maggie talk about that?"

"Yeah," Roscoe said. "The two of them took off one morning. Paddington was a straight guy, but apparently he was a pretty wild pilot. Maggie was with them in the kitchen when they got this idea to fly up there on the spur of the moment. Maggie heard the wife say, 'Shouldn't we file a flight plan?' or something like that, but Paddington just shrugged it off. They were supposed to be back in four days. The next day,

Maggie remembered, she read about big storms that were over the Atlantic, but she didn't think too much about it. Four days came and went and they didn't get any word. But they waited. They worked for the Paddingtons, so they waited. After a couple of weeks, they asked a few questions and found out the Paddingtons never got to the big seal protest. It was another couple of months before they decided that the plane must have crashed and maybe they could cash in on it. They started small at first, signing Mrs. Paddington's name to checks, paying bills, stuff like that—small stuff, so that if the Paddingtons showed up one day, they could just say they were trying to keep things running smoothly. Finally they decided they could get away with it forever, but it'd be easier if they moved where no one knew them."

"They might have gotten away with it forever," Chico said, "if they hadn't gotten greedy."

"Greed is the poison of the human spirit," Trace said unctuously. "Some persons within earshot would be well-advised to remember that."

"Stuff it, Trace," Chico said.

"Were they married?" Trace asked.

"Ferd and Maggie? Yeah," Roscoe said. "They came from some small town in Minnesota. Ferd was a high-school janitor and Maggie was a student and they got married after he knocked her up. But she lost the baby. She's kind of afraid of him."

Trace rubbed the fading bruise under his left eye. "I can't imagine why," he said.

"Anyway," Roscoe said, "I just came over to thank you. Tomorrow, when we take your statement, Tracy, let's not say anything about the burglary that wasn't a burglary. My life is complicated enough as it is."

"That suits me fine," Trace said.

After the policeman left Trace said to Chico, "It all sounded so easy when you told about it. Why couldn't I do it?"

"Because you were drunk most of the time you were here," Chico said. "You think you function just as well when you're drunk, but let me tell you, as someone who's slept next to you for four years, that's a pipe dream."

"Well, that's behind us now," Trace said. "Moderation is my new game plan from here on in. For instance, to celebrate, I might have one vodka tonight. Just one."

He looked around for the waitress, but when she came, Chico said, "He'll have another wine."

Trace woke up the next morning when Chico came back into the room. She walked to the bedside and dropped a newspaper onto his bare chest.

"You're a star," she said.

He willed his eyes to open. "What's that you say?"

"There's a big story in there." She perched

on the side of the bed, opened the newspaper, and read, 'Lt. Sam Roscoe of Westport police said the major credit for breaking the murder and fraud case should go to Devlin Tracy, an investigator for the Garrison Fidelity Insurance Company, who had been looking into the spurious Paddington insurance claim for the past week."

Trace vaulted out of bed. "Time to go," he said. "How fast can you pack?"

"Hold on. What's the hurry?" Chico said. "I like this town."

"That story," Trace said. "There are probably a lot more just like it in a whole bunch of papers."

"So what?"

"So this. So my ex-wife sees it, and before I know it, she's camping outside our room with What's-his-name and the girl. Time to get back to Las Vegas."

"That doesn't frighten me," Chico said.

"And my mother. She might see it and decide to come up here and visit me."

"I'll call the airlines," Chico said.

Driving to the airport after dictating a brief statement to a police stenographer, Trace told Chico, "I want you to know that I think it was real nice of you to offer me that money to help with the restaurant. Even if I won't need it now because of my fee."

"Thank you," Chico said. "When I talked to Sarge, he said you sounded really depressed. I thought if it meant that much to you, I'd better help."

"Well, thank you," Trace said. "You justified my faith in humanity."

"What are friends for?" Chico said. And a few seconds later, she said, "But I'm just glad that I won't have to sink any of *my* money down that dry well."

At the airport, Trace finally got around to calling Walter Marks.

"Where have you been?" Marks demanded. "I've been calling you for days."

"Hey, read the papers," Trace said. "I'm a big hero. Garrison Fidelity is famous. At my press conference, I said I owe all my success to you."

"That'll be the day."

"Groucho, don't you think some congratulations are in order?" Trace asked.

"For what?"

"For what? For the Paddington case. For saving the company two million dollars," Trace said.

"For bullshit," Marks shouted.

"What?"

"Paddington's dead. You proved that, I guess. He died in an accident. So that means we're gonna have to pay two million to somebody. If not his wife, probably some goddamn animal shelter. We'll just have to wait till his will is read. All because you had to go and prove that he was dead."

"I can't believe you're saying this."

"I didn't want Paddington dead," Marks said. "I wanted him alive and a fraud. Dead, he costs us two million. Trace, I hate you. We're gonna have to pay."

"Goddammit, Groucho, I saved you from paying the wrong person. You want people to think Gone Fishing is an easy mark?"

"Well, you saved us nothing, don't forget that."

"You think I did all this work for dogshit?" Trace snapped.

"I don't know what you did it for. Not for us, that's for sure."

"I'm sending you a bill for my fee," Trace said.

"Keep it small," Marks said.

"I'm sending you a bill, and if you give me any static, I'm going to the press. I'm a media hero now, Groucho. I'll make you look like a fool. Well, God already did that. I'll think of something."

"Just keep the bill reasonable," Marks said.

Trace hung up and returned to his seat in the waiting room next to Chico.

"How'd it go?" she asked.

"The usual," Trace said. "Groucho's trying to chisel me again. Nothing to worry about."

* * *

Back in their Las Vegas condominium, Chico checked the telephone tapes and told Trace he had a message from his friend Eddie in New Jersey.

Trace called him and said, "How much is it now, you goddamn bandit?"

"I've got good news," Eddie said.

"Let me sit down first. Okay, go ahead," Trace said.

"I thought about what you said, so I talked to a new contractor. Trace, we've got termites."

"I'm waiting for the good news."

"The building's not structurally sound," Eddie said.

"I'm still waiting."

"But the contractor who found the termites, he wants to buy it anyway. He says he's got a lot of guys out of work and he can fix it for himself on the cheap."

"Where's the good news?" Trace said.

"He offered to buy us out," Eddie said.

"How much profit will I make?"

"He'll give us ninety cents on the dollar," Eddie said.

"That means I'm out of this deal but I lose four thousand dollars?" Trace said.

"That's right."

"That *is* good news," Trace said. "Send me my check right away."

"I will."

"And, Eddie, if you run into any more deals . . ."

"Yes," Eddie said.

"File them where the sun doesn't shine."

Exciting Fiction from SIGNET

*Prices slightly higher in Canada

Buy them at your local
bookstore or use coupon
on next page for ordering.

Thrilling Reading from SIGNET

(0451)

☐ **ON WINGS OF EAGLES** by Ken Follett. (131517—$4.50)*

☐ **THE MAN FROM ST. PETERSBURG** by Ken Follett. (124383—$3.95)*

☐ **EYE OF THE NEEDLE** by Ken Follett. (124308—$3.95)*

☐ **TRIPLE** by Ken Follett. (127900—$3.95)*

☐ **THE KEY TO REBECCA** by Ken Follett. (127889—$3.95)*

☐ **EXOCET** by Jack Higgins. (130448—$3.95)†

☐ **DARK SIDE OF THE STREET** by Jack Higgins. (128613—$2.95)†

☐ **TOUCH THE DEVIL** by Jack Higgins. (124685—$3.95)†

☐ **THE TEARS OF AUTUMN** by Charles McCarry. (131282—$3.95)°

☐ **THE LAST SUPPER** by Charles McCarry. (128575—$3.50)°

☐ **FAMILY TRADE** by James Carroll. (123255—$3.95)*

*Prices slightly higher in Canada

†Not available in Canada

Buy them at your local bookstore or use this convenient coupon for ordering.

NEW AMERICAN LIBRARY,
P.O. Box 999, Bergenfield, New Jersey 07621

Please send me the books I have checked above. I am enclosing $＿＿＿＿＿
(please add $1.00 to this order to cover postage and handling). Send check
or money order—no cash or C.O.D.'s. Prices and numbers are subject to change
without notice.

Name ＿＿＿＿＿＿＿＿＿＿＿＿＿＿＿＿＿＿＿＿＿＿＿＿＿＿＿＿＿＿

Address ＿＿＿＿＿＿＿＿＿＿＿＿＿＿＿＿＿＿＿＿＿＿＿＿＿＿＿＿

City ＿＿＿＿＿＿＿＿＿＿ State ＿＿＿＿＿＿ Zip Code ＿＿＿＿＿＿

Allow 4-6 weeks for delivery.
This offer is subject to withdrawal without notice.

JOIN THE *SIGNET MYSTERY* READERS' PANEL

Help us bring you more of the books you like by filling out this survey and mailing it in today.

1. Book Title: _____

2. Using the scale below, how would you rate this book or the following features? Please write in one number from 0-10 in the spaces provided.

POOR	NOT SO GOOD		O.K.			GOOD		EXCEL-LENT
0	1	2	3	4	5	6	7	8	9	10

RATIN■

Overall opinion of book .... ____
Scene on Front Cover .... ____

3. What are your two favorite magazines?
   A. _____
   B. _____

4. Do you belong to a *mystery* book club?
   (   ) Yes   (   ) No

5. About how many mystery paperbacks do you buy ea■ month? _____

6. What is your education?
   (   ) High School (or less)   (   ) 4 yrs. college
   (   ) 2 yrs. college   (   ) Post Graduate

7. Age _____   8. Sex: (   ) Male   (   ) Female

9. Occupation: _____

Please Print Name: _____

Address: _____

City: _____ State: _____ Zip: _____

Phone #: (   ) _____

Thank you. Please send to New American Library, Rese■ Dept., 1633 Broadway, New York, NY 10019.